My Love's Keeper

Rochelle Alers

Domhan Books

ISBN: 1-58345-970-7 paper
1-58345-971-5 Pdf
1-58345-972-3 Adobe
1-58345-973-1 Glass

Published by Domhan Books
9511 Shore Road, Suite 514
Brooklyn New York 11209
www.domhanbooks.com
cover art by Stacey King, Crystal Moon
Design, www.crystalmoondesign.com

Printed by Lightning Source
Distributed by Ingram Book Group

Nicole Moore felt the ravages of frustration whenever she was near Zachary Regan. She wanted to belong to him totally. Zachary found this beautiful woman more desirable than any other woman he had ever known. But could her love for him break through the barrier of fear that held him captive?

Rochelle Alers

Native New Yorker Rochelle Alers now resides in a picturesque fishing village on Long Island with her family where she draws inspiration to write her sensual novels and short stories. A former pre-school teacher, she has changed careers for the corporate world.

Rochelle holds degrees in sociology and psychology, which help to provide her with what she needs to create sexy, sophisticated men and women who dare to risk everything for love.

Her interests include music, art, gourmet cooking, and traveling. She utilizes all of her hobbies in her novels, as evidenced by the exotic locales in the extremely popular HIDEAWAY Series.

A prolific writer, she is the author of more than a dozen novels and short stories -- several which have been translated into foreign languages, as well as optioned for a made-for-television movie.

Also by the author

Careless Whispers
Gentle Yearning
Heaven Sent
Harvest Moon
Holiday Cheer
Rosie's Curl & Weave
Summer Magic
Vows
Reckless Surrender
Hidden Agenda
"Hearts of Gold" in *Love Letters*,
Arabesque's 1997 Valentine's anthology
Home Sweet Home
Hideaway
Happily Ever After

Chapter One

Heads turned and eyes shifted to the tall woman following the maitre d' to a table at the rear of the restaurant. The fitted black knit turtleneck dress outlined the incredible slimness of her five foot, ten inch figure. The hem ended two inches above her knees, offering admiring male glances a full view of long shapely legs and feet encased in sheer black hose and black suede pumps.

Her thick, glossy dark brown chemically-straightened hair was pulled into an elaborate chignon on a long, graceful neck. Nicole Moore's expressive clear brown eyes crinkled in a smile as they came to rest on a brilliant pair in a startling jade green. Her smile faltered a bit when she caught the obsidian stare of the man sitting with Adam Moore. The slight frown that touched her brow vanished quickly. The man sitting with her brother wore a wide gold band on the third finger of his right hand. She thought Adam had asked her to dinner with the sole purpose of introducing her to one of his single friends or business associates. Fortunately for her, this man was married.

Adam rose to his feet, extending both arms. "You are definitely the most beautiful woman to walk the face of the earth."

Nicole offered her cheek for a kiss, grasping Adam's hands. "You're biased, Adam Moore." She touched her lips to her brother's smooth jaw, then wiped away the smudge of orange lip color near his generous male mouth.

Adam held her at arm's length, grinning smugly at his dining partner who stood staring down at Nicole. "Did I lie to you, Zack? Can you believe this incredibly beautiful woman is my sister? Nicole, this is Zachary Regan. Zack, Nicole."

She pulled out of Adam's embrace and extended her right hand, smiling. "Hello, Zachary. Don't believe everything he says. He's been known to lie on occasion."

Zachary Regan's expression was impassive. Midnight eyes behind oval gold-wired glasses swept slowly over her face. He took her fingers, holding them gently within his larger hand.

"He didn't lie, Nicole." His voice was soft, with a trace of a midwest drawl. "You are exquisite."

Nicole nodded, extracting her fingers. She smiled at Adam when he pulled out a chair to seat her. She wasn't vain about her looks. She had grown up basking in male attention, her father and Adam continually reminding her of her natural feminine attractiveness and giving her the confidence she needed when she towered over all of her girlfriends and some boys as an adolescent.

"I hope you don't mind that I invited Zack to join us," Adam said. "Every time I come to New York he's either out of town or busy on a project. Zack's the architect who designed my house," he explained.

Nicole looked up from her menu and stared at the man seated across from her, unable to conceal her surprise. She would not have thought Zachary Regan was an architect. If he was Adam's friend she would have presupposed him to be an attorney also; it appeared as if all of her brother's friends were attorneys.

"You are truly an artistic genius to have transformed that shell of a house into a magnificent showplace," Nicole said, complimenting Zachary.

Eighteen months before Adam had bought an abandoned, dilapidated farmhouse in Arlington, Virginia.

Zachary gave her a perceptible nod. "It's always easier when you begin with a shell," he replied modestly.

"Don't let Zack's modesty fool you, Nick," Adam countered with a broad smile. "The man has won numerous awards for his designs. Even before he graduated from Howard, most of the major firms were after him."

"Who did you decide to go with?"

Zachary arched a thick black eyebrow. "The one who made me the best offer. My perks included a full graduate scholarship to Yale, an apartment, car and a generous stipend."

"Good for you," Nicole replied.

She perused the menu after taking a surreptitious glance at Zachary Regan. His bookish appearance was deceptively attractive. His coarse hair was close cut, closer than her conservative brother's, and brushed back off a high, intelligent forehead. His skin was smooth and clear, the color reminiscent of golden-brown autumn leaves. High cheekbones, a bold nose and a full, strongly sculpted and totally masculine mouth made for an arresting face.

Adam waited until the waiter had taken Nicole's selection before saying, "You wear your vacation well."

Nicole touched her suntanned cheeks. The Caribbean sun had darkened her tawny skin, highlighting the gold flecks in her large eyes.

"It was wonderful." Her mouth turned down in a frown. "But I had to come back."

Zachary took in her distressed expression. "Where did you go?"

"St. Thomas." She sighed heavily. "Spending two weeks in the Caribbean in January is what helps me to survive New York winters."

"You don't like cold weather?" Zachary questioned.

Nicole wrinkled her nose. "I *hate* it."

Zachary smiled at her, flashing a deep dimple in his right cheek. "Then you never would've survived growing up in Chicago. The wind blowing off Lake Michigan made it feel as if you were in the Antarctic instead of the United States."

"I take it you like the cold weather?" she asked.

"I'm used to it," Zachary answered.

The sommelier approached the table and uncorked a bottle of wine, filling three glasses with a pale blush liquid. Nicole recognized the label as her favorite. Whenever Adam flew into New York City on business he made it a practice to share either lunch or dinner with her before returning to Washington, D. C.

Adam raised his glass in a toast. "I'd like to toast my good friend's business success," he said to Zachary, "and my sister's future. May she fall in love, get married and give her mother a grandchild. In that order, of course."

"Adam! How could you!" Nicole gasped in embarrassment.

Adam took a sip of wine, unmoved by Nicole's outburst. "The woman haunts me relentlessly about grandchildren. You don't get to hear it because she knows you refuse to discuss it. But I'm the *good* son, so I listen and 'yes' her to death."

Zachary glanced down at Nicole's slender ringless fingers. "Do you find the idea of getting married distasteful, Nicole?"

She tilted her chin slightly, giving him a sidelong glance. "No. I just haven't found the right man."

Adam winked at Zachary. "He doesn't exist."

She frowned at Adam. "That's not true."

Adam loosened the navy blue tie under the collar of his stark white shirt. "Whether it's true or not, I don't intend to get married for another two years. So you'd better stop dragging your feet, little sister."

Nicole sipped her wine, the cool liquid sliding down the back of her throat. She refused to discuss her mother's idiosyncrasies in front of a stranger.

She was thirty-three and Adam thirty-nine, yet neither of them had come close to marrying and producing a grandchild for their mother; and Adam wasn't much different from Margaret Moore. Both of them planned their lives right down to the smallest detail. Adam had always wanted to become a politician, and he knew the quickest way was through law. He had secured a position as a partner in a prestigious Washington firm and planned to seek an elected position in government within the next two years; and that left sixty-four-year old Margaret Moore in a perpetual state of anxiety, unable to understand why at least one of her children hadn't given her one grandchild.

Nicole glanced up from under her lashes at Zachary. His slight smile indicated he was amused by the interchange between her and Adam.

The waiter returned to the table and leaned over to whisper something in Adam's ear.

He nodded and pushed back from the table. "Please excuse me. I have a telephone call."

Zachary gave Nicole his full attention, visually examining the perfection of her face. Adam hadn't lied; Nicole Moore was the most beautiful woman he had ever seen.

And he also wondered why she hadn't married. "Does Adam usually needle you about being single?" he asked Nicole.

Nicole traced the rim of her wineglass with a forefinger. "Only when my mother sinks in her claws and refuses to let go." Her head came up and she smiled at Zachary. "I live too far for Mother to monitor my social life."

"Adam said that you manage to keep quite busy with your work at the family center."

She regarded him with a speculative gaze. "It appears as if Adam told you a lot about me."

Zachary shrugged broad shoulders under a charcoal gray suit jacket. "Only that you're a social worker and that you're quite beautiful." Lowering his chin, he stared at her with his mysterious black eyes. "You do know that you're a beautiful woman."

Zachary Regan was a married man, and because he was she chose her words carefully. "I've heard it before."

He gave her a half-smile. "And you believe it?"

"It depends on who's saying it."

His smile faded. "Why do you say that?"

"Some men will say anything when they want something from a woman."

"Would I be included in that group?"

"No," she replied quickly.

His gaze lowered with his voice. "Why not?"

"Because you're married," Nicole said flippantly.

"I'm not married, Nicole."

Zachary successfully concealed a smile when he saw Nicole's delicate jaw drop. He was certain the flush stealing across her high cheekbones was from uneasiness rather than applied color.

She blinked several times. "But—you're wearing a wedding band."

Zachary laced his long fingers together on the top of the pale gray tablecloth. "I'm a widower. My wife died six years ago," he explained.

"I'm sorry, Zachary," Nicole said in a broken whisper.

"To hear that I'm a widower, and therefore single?" he teased.

Nicole realized he was teasing her, and she let out her breath slowly. "No, not at all. I'm sorry you lost your wife."

He picked up his glass and took a swallow of wine, peering at her over the fluted rim. He brought the glass down slowly. "You're safe from me, Nicole."

"How's that?" Nicole was still trying to recover from Zachary's disclosure that he wasn't married.

"I don't intend to marry again."

Something in his tone touched Nicole. There was a cold hardness in his statement. "Maybe you'll change your mind one of these days. A woman will come along and you won't be able to imagine your life without her," she predicted.

"I doubt that," he stated emphatically. "Right now I have to concentrate on raising my children and keeping my company solvent."

"How many children do you have?"

"Three. Katherine's twelve and my twin sons, Daniel and David, are eight."

That meant when Zachary's wife passed away she'd left him with three babies. "Who looks after them?"

"I have a live-in housekeeper. There was a time when I changed housekeepers on a weekly basis until I found Henrietta. The children like her and she seems to be fond of them."

Adam returned to the table, tightening his tie. Nicole felt his controlled tension when he touched her shoulder. "I have to leave."

She half-rose from her chair. "What's the matter?" Her gaze searched her brother's dark green eyes frantically.

"It's all right, baby. It's not Mom or Dad. The deal I've been working on just hit a snag. It looks like I'm going to be up for the night."

Nicole stood up, the top of her head coming to Adam's nose. Both of them had inherited their father's towering height. The fingers of her right hand smoothed back the lines of worry in his forehead. "You're pushing too hard, Adam."

He kissed her forehead. "After this merger, I'm coming up for a vacation. Springtime in the Big Apple has always appealed to me. I have to go. A driver's waiting to take me to the airport." Reaching into the pocket on his trousers, he withdrew several large bills and dropped them on the table. "Both of you stay and have dinner."

Zachary rose to his feet, his head level with Adam's. He picked up the bills and pushed them into Adam's hand. I'll take care of it this time. I'll also see that Nicole gets home safely."

Adam kissed Nicole, shook Zachary's hand, then he was gone. She stood staring at her brother's departing back until Zachary touched her arm.

"I don't know about you, but I'm starved, Nicole. I've existed on black coffee all day."

She nodded, thinking of her numerous cups of coffee and a hastily eaten tuna salad hours before.

Zachary seated her, lingering over her head and inhaling the cloying scent of her perfume. The sandalwood and jasmine fragrance epitomized Nicole Moore: warm, rich, lingering and subtle, yet persistent. It had been a long time—too long—since all of his senses had been assaulted by a woman. And he hadn't thought that woman would be his fraternity brother's younger sister.

Zachary retook his own seat and refilled their glasses with more of the Zinfandel. He chanced a quick glance at Nicole's solemn expression.

"You're worried about Adam working too hard." It came out like a statement rather than a question.

"Adam has always pushed himself to the limit."

"He says the same thing about you," Zachary countered.

"That's only when I'm working on a project."

"What project are you working on now?"

Nicole experienced a jolt of excitement. As associate director of an East Harlem family services agency, her responsibilities had become one of program coordinator. And in the four years since she had worked for the agency, she had instituted three community-based programs that involved the youth with various business and religious organizations.

"I've begun a project called Vocation Bound. I've tried to match high school students with various businesses in the East Harlem area with apprenticeship positions. Unfortunately many kids don't know what they want to do after they graduate, if they graduate at all. We're working with several guidance counselors who conduct their own vocational surveys and together we try to steer students toward their areas of interest or expertise."

Zachary shifted his eyebrows in surprise. "I like your project."

Nicole registered his sincerity. "Thank you. The support has been quite positive."

Zachary took in her animated expression. Her clear eyes sparkled as her lush mouth softened in a smile. Her dimpled chin was enchanting and sexy. For that fact, everything about Nicole was sexy. He hadn't missed her fluid walk; her walk reminded him of a runway model's seductive strut. He also hadn't missed how the knitted material of her dress clung to her body, accentuating her hips and small rounded breasts. The concealing black dress was more provocative than one that would've revealed expanses of bare flesh.

He didn't know why, but Nicole bothered him; bothered him a great deal more than he wanted to be bothered. And he couldn't help himself when he asked, "Do you have a candidate for an architectural and design firm?"

As their eyes met, she felt a surge of warmth. She hadn't expected to solicit Zachary's input, but he was making it easy for her.

"Where are you located?"

"Ninety-third, between Fifth and Madison. We occupy a three-story townhouse.

Nicole felt her joy dissipating quickly. "You're out of the geographic boundaries."

Zachary waved an exquisitely formed large hand. "As project coordinator, can't you move the boundaries to suit your program?"

She peered up at him through a sweep of long lashes. "I'm certain I can," she drawled in a husky voice.

"Then it's settled."

He felt a quickening in the lower part of his body at her seductive stare. He knew further association with Nicole Moore beyond dinner was courting danger, but he couldn't help himself. He had to see her again. Perhaps after he saw her a second time, he would rid himself of the spell she had woven without being aware of it.

"I'll be in touch with you in a few days. I'll let you know what to look for in a candidate. Then my secretary will set up an interview schedule.''

Nicole couldn't believe it had been that easy. ''Why are you doing this, Zachary?''

There was a pregnant silence while their waiter served Nicole a puree of leek and potato soup, and placed a plate of mixed greens and baby lettuce with warm goat cheese on the table for Zachary.

''It was too late to cancel Mr. Moore's appetizer,'' the waiter apologized. He set down a bowl filled with large boiled shrimp on a bed of cracked ice. The distinctive and pungent aroma of cocktail sauce wafted in the air.

''It's all right,'' Zachary said, giving the waiter a reassuring smile and a nod of dismissal.

''You ask me why, Nicole?'' he continued. Doesn't someone have to lend a hand, give back a little something to our children for the future?'' A faraway look filled his eyes with sadness. ''My parents died in a fire when I was ten. It was an aunt who took me in and raised me as her son. As a single woman she supported herself running a boardinghouse in a tough Chicago neighborhood.

''Her roomers were transients, and I got to see every side of human life imaginable. She preached relentlessly, 'God bless the dead, Zachary. Your daddy and mama wanted the best for you, just like I want you to make somethin' out of yourself. You don't have to walk more than fifty feet beyond this porch to see the world. It's all right here in this boardinghouse. Some of my roomers are hardworkin' folks who'll never 'mount to nothin'; but then some of them don't want no better. Don't be like them. Don't disappoint me, son. Make me proud of you. Do it. Not for yourself, but for your dead mama and daddy. Make me proud.' I thought about her words, and I was determined to make her proud.

"She did most of the cooking and cleaning, struggling to keep her head above water. And she sacrificed her hard-earned money to give me art lessons. She cared about me, Nicole. And because she did I tried harder. I made the grades and managed a partial scholarship to Howard. From there it was easy. I'm not wealthy, yet my children will have it a great deal easier than I did. It should be that way with each succeeding generation. It should be easier."

If Adam and Zachary were friends, then he knew how easy it had been for them. As the children of a dental surgeon and a school teacher, Nicole and Adam only had to select the college of their choice, not concerning themselves about the cost of tuition, books or room and board.

Yet it had been different for Zachary as it was for many of the children growing up in the East Harlem neighborhood where Nicole worked and now lived. She'd moved into her high-rise apartment building along Manhattan's First Avenue six months before, and for the first time in all of the years she had worked for the agency, she felt as if she had become an integral part of the community.

"Where have you placed your apprentices?" he questioned.

"A small dance studio has offered a girl a year of free instruction; we've placed two students with a restaurateur who specializes in Italian cuisine. Several young boys have been hired as mechanics at a service station and we've managed to get a few hired as bookkeepers, secretaries and receptionists at a number of walk-in medical clinics."

Zachary toyed with his salad, unable to tear his gaze away from Nicole's face. Her beauty was merely a foil for a woman who claimed intelligence as an inherent gift. And he also sensed her strength; a strength that did not minimize her femininity.

They lingered over dinner, savoring expertly prepared dishes of succulent poached salmon and veal marsala. Both of them declined dessert and coffee.

Nicole was offered her first unobscured look at Zachary Regan when he helped her into her coat. He was as tall as Adam but broader. The lines of his charcoal gray suit were tailored to fit the breadth of his shoulders and long legs. Everything about him was tasteful. He was a perfect role model for a young man or woman who would intern at his architectural and design firm.

She pulled the collar to her coat up around her ears as she left the restaurant with Zachary. A frigid wind off the East River searched through the layers of wool, biting and stinging with a relentless vengeance.

Zachary reached for her gloved hand and held it tightly. They walked half a block, then he pulled her close to his side, sharing some of his body's heat.

"Look on the bright side, Nicole," Zachary said against her ear, his warm breath adding heat to her numbed cheek. "Spring is only two months away."

Nicole curved an arm around his waist, tucking her head against his shoulder. "I don't know if I'll survive until then," she mumbled into the cashmere pile of his topcoat.

He steered her down another block and into an indoor garage. He handed the parking attendant a receipt, then cradled Nicole's face between his hands. "I'll have you home soon," he promised softly.

She met his steady gaze behind the lenses of his glasses and smiled. His nearness soothed her, made her feel comfortable; more comfortable than she had ever felt with any man. She didn't know whether it was because he was Adam's friend, or because their relationship would be viewed as platonic. Nicole wasn't ready to give up her independence and marry, and Zachary had made it plain that he wasn't interested in becoming involved with her, or with any woman. Knowing this permitted her to lower her defenses.

Five minutes later Nicole sat beside Zachary in a two-seater, taupe-colored Mercedes coupe, the powerful engine's heat warming her stiff limbs. The scent of leather mingled with the lime of Zachary's after-shave. The combination was heady; heady masculine cleanliness.

Despite the bitterly cold winter weather, people were walking briskly along the frozen sidewalks. Billows of heat rose from under the pavement as Manhattan resembled the images filmmakers created when they depicted a futuristic world. Through the closed windows, the sounds of honking automobile horns, blaring radios and raucous laughter could still be heard. It was a cold mid-January night, yet the city was still awake and pulsing with a life all its own.

Zachary decided to drive up Madison Avenue instead of taking the F.D.R. Drive uptown. He didn't want the night to end. He wanted to savor Nicole Moore's presence a bit longer.

"The next building is mine," Nicole said, pointing and directing Zachary to her building amid the others in the high-rise complex. He found a parking space along a side street and came around the car to help her out.

Nicole barely had time to gather her handbag when he swept her up into his arms. "What are you doing?" she gasped, trying to retain her balance as she caught his neck.

Zachary smiled down at her. "Keeping you warm."

"Put me down, Zachary Regan." She looked around to see if anyone saw them.

"When I get you to your building." His fingers tightened under her knees. His strong grip wouldn't permit her to free herself.

"Put me down now," Nicole ordered against his throat.

"Yes, ma'am." They had reached the front door to the building. He set her on her feet and held out his hand. "Your keys, please."

Nicole handed him the keys and waited for him to open the door. She retrieved them, opened her mailbox and extracted a stack of junk mail, magazines and bills. She watched Zachary punch the button to the elevators.

He glanced around the lobby. "Nice building. Have you lived here long?"

She stared at his profile. "I moved in six months ago. Where do you live?"

He turned back to her. "In Oyster Bay. That's about thirty miles from here."

"Long Island?"

"Yes. Long Island."

The doors to the elevator opened. Nicole stepped in, Zachary following her. She pushed the button for the twenty-second floor and stared at the doors rather than Zachary. She had tried to ignore him, but that wasn't possible. The close confines of his small car, and now the elevator made her more than aware of his compelling magnetism. Zachary Regan was not a man a woman could ignore that easily.

The doors opened and their footsteps were muffled in the thick pile of the carpeting lining the hallway. Again Zachary reached for her keys when she stopped in front of the door to her apartment. He unlocked the two locks, stepped into the entry, then motioned for her to enter.

The wall-to-wall drapes had not been drawn and the panoramic scene of the bridges spanning Manhattan with the other boroughs lit up the nighttime skyline.

Zachary was drawn across the expansive living room to the window. He stood motionless, taking in the breathtaking view. "Everything looks so clean, so beautiful and so peaceful from here." He turned, watching Nicole remove her coat and kick off her shoes. "Your place is magnificent."

She gave him a warm smile. "Thank you."

His practiced eye took in the priceless furnishings scattered through the living/dining area. "I see that you're into antiques."

"I inherited most pieces from my grandmother."

He pulled a hand from the pocket of his slacks and gingerly touched the top of a desk positioned near a wall of built-in shelves.

"Did you get *this* from your grandmother, too?"

Nicole should not have been surprised that Zachary recognized the most expensive piece of furniture she owned. He was a trained artist, therefore he was familiar with all of the art styles and their periods.

"No. I picked that up at an auction."

He ran a finger over the faded golden-hued and patined mahogany surface. "How high did the bidding go?"

She wound her arms around her middle. "Too high." It was the only time she had ever been that reckless and impulsive.

Zachary pulled his gaze away from the Adams desk. "But not so high that you didn't buy it."

"I had to have it." She'd promised herself that she would never divulge what she had paid for the desk. It was a secret she would carry to her grave.

"I know an antique dealer out on Long Island who carries some wonderful little *items* that might interest you," Zachary said with a dimpled smile. "When you feel you 'have to have' something else, let me know and she'll arrange a private showing. That'll also give me an opportunity to show you where I live."

She wasn't ready to visit Zachary's home. Meeting with him at his office or her own would be all she could take of him--for now; and for a man who didn't want to become involved with any woman he should not have been that virile. Everything about him was masculine and compelling.

"I'll let you know," she replied, not committing herself.

Right now Nicole knew she couldn't afford to buy anything that wasn't essential for her day-to-day existence. She had overspent for gifts when on vacation, and it would be several months before she could splurge on anything deemed frivolous.

Nicole steepled her fingers, bringing them to her mouth. For an instant, she felt a rush of awkwardness, and she had no way of knowing that Zachary was undergoing the same emotion.

"I'll need a number where I can reach you as soon as I'm able to recruit a few candidates for your firm," she said softly.

Zachary reached into the breast pocket of his suit jacket and withdrew a brass case. He handed her a business card. "You can call me at any time. If I'm not in the office, leave a message with my secretary. She'll always be able to reach me. I know where to contact you," he said before she could offer him her number.

Nicole had no doubt about that. Zachary had installed a mobile telephone in his car. She extended her hand, smiling. "It's been a most enjoyable evening, Zachary."

He took the proffered hand, examining her manicured fingernails. The pleasure has been mine, Nicole."

She pulled her fingers from his loose grip. "Good night, Zachary."

He held her gaze before her lids lowered, shadowing clear brown eyes that reminded him of burnt-sienna. "I'll be in touch."

The four words lingered and replayed over and over in her head long after she'd shut and locked the door behind Zachary Regan's retreating figure.

"I'm looking forward to it," she finally whispered as she made her way to her bedroom.

Chapter Two

Nicole slipped the tortoiseshell pins from the twist of hair on her nape, releasing a wealth of thick coiling strands. She undressed, dropping her dress, a full slip and panty hose on the mahogany chest at the foot of a large queen-size four-poster bed. As with most of the other pieces of furniture in her apartment, the bed and chest had belonged to her grandmother. Nicole could also boast that several mismatched silver items she owned had been in her family for more than one hundred thirty-five years. She hoped that one day she would own her own home where she could openly display her heirlooms.

She checked her answering machine for messages and saw a lighted zero. She hadn't expected to hear from Carson Bates so soon after he'd taken off for a trip to the west coast. He was to spend three days in San Francisco, lecturing to a group of fellow cardiologists, then return to New York in time for a Super Bowl party he had asked her to help host for their mutual friends.

Nicole had met Dr. Carson Bates at a fund-raising luncheon a week before Thanksgiving, and it was only after he'd left several messages with her secretary at the center did she attempt to return his calls. It took only one date to realize that Carson still had not recovered from the break up of his ten-year marriage to his childhood sweetheart. And she was realistic enough to know that any serious involvement with Carson would result in heartbreak. She was not ready to become a substitute for an ex-wife Carson loved unselfishly.

Nicole picked up the telephone and dialed a number she knew as well as her own.

"Yes," came a throaty feminine voice.

"Vera, it's Nicole."

"What's up, Nick? Don't tell me Carson is cancelling the party for Sunday."

Nicole flopped down on the bed, pulling a pillow under her head. "No, it's nothing like that. I want you to check out a few students when you go to school tomorrow."

There was a low groan from Vera. "What are you up to now?"

Nicole could imagine Vera's frown. Once Vera left the halls of the high school where she worked as a guidance counselor, she never wanted to hear the word *students*.

"I need some background on one or two art students."

"Who are they for?"

Nicole picked up the business card bearing Zachary Regan's name. "Regan and Associates, AIA."

"Say what?"

"It's an architectural and design firm."

"Where did you find this fat pigeon, Nick?"

Nicole laughed into the receiver. "He found me, Vera. Zachary Regan is the architect who redesigned the interiors of Adam's house."

There was a noticeable pause from Vera. Nicole was aware that her best friend was still in love with Adam.

"You saw Adam?" came Vera's small inquiry.

"He was in town for a few hours. I shared a drink with him, but that was all because he had to return to Washington."

Vera let out a loud sigh. "I'll see what I can do for you. Look, Nick, it's late. I'd better turn in. I have a departmental breakfast meeting tomorrow."

"Thanks, Vera."

"Anything for you, Nick."

The line went dead and Nicole hung up. She had warned Vera when she first met Adam not to lose her heart to him. But Vera, like so many other women, ignored her warning. Vera and Adam managed a year-long shuttle liaison, then Vera was jolted into reality when she issued her ultimatum: she wanted to become Mrs. Adam Moore.

Nicole became sister, counselor and emotional lifeline to Vera Walker during her bouts of depression. It was only recently that Vera had begun dating again.

Swinging her legs over the side of the bed, Nicole headed for the bathroom to begin her nightly ritual of cleansing her face, brushing her hair and relaxing in a tub filled with bath salts in her favorite fragrance. It was a practice she had developed at twenty-one, and she had never missed a night, no matter how late the hour or how fatigued she felt. The ritual was indicative of how orderly her life had become; and Nicole did not want anything or anyone to upset the balance.

She returned to the bedroom forty-five minutes later and crawled into bed. She finished reading the newspaper, watched the late edition of the nightly news, then pushed the button on the remote control, turning off the television.

Nicole reached over and flicked off the bedside lamp. In the instant before darkness enveloped the space, her gaze caught the small rectangle of parchment with dark blue letters emblazoned with the Regan and Associates' logo lying near the telephone. The memory of Zachary carrying her from his car to her apartment building wrung a smile from her. But the way she'd felt in his arms banished the smile. His warmth, strength and the clean scent of soap and cologne on his smooth jaw had been a sensual feast; a feast she wanted to partake of again and again.

You're safe from me, Nicole.

His words attacked her. Zachary Regan was taboo, verboten and definitely off-limits. But that did not stop a little part of her from wanting to see him again.

She had become accustomed to men pursuing her, not her pursuing them. Unknowingly, Zachary had just reversed that trend.

It was another two days before Zachary attempted to call Nicole Moore. It took that long for him to berate himself for thinking with his gonads rather than his gray matter, and he knew it was more than Nicole's face and body that made him want to see and touch her again.

He wanted to see her smile, hear her voice with a lingering trace of a Virginia drawl and watch the fluidity of her body when she walked. He wanted to know if he'd imagined the way she held her head when she looked up at him from under her lashes; and most of all he wanted to relive the feel of her silken skin. Cradling her face between his hands had ignited sparks of passion he thought had died with Julie.

As a widower he had not been relegated to a state of celibacy. He saw a woman; a divorced woman who had mutually agreed that their physical relationship be free from any emotional entanglements. This arrangement suited him well, because there was no room in his life for love and marriage.

Zachary pushed his hands into the pockets of a pair of faded laundered jeans and rocked back on the heels of his low-heeled black boots, letting out his breath slowly as he examined the intricate lines and curves of the plans on the drafting table. Hunter Manor was complete. It had taken him ten months to design the house for a Texas developer.

"Miss Moore is on your private line," came his secretary's voice through the speaker on Zachary's desk.

Zachary moved over to the desk and pressed a button. "Thank you, Lisa."

He sat down on the edge of the desk, staring at the telephone. He'd called the center on Wednesday and was told that Nicole would not return to the office until Friday. He wondered what had kept her away from her work for two days.

Leaning over, he picked up the receiver. "Good morning."

"Good morning to you," Nicole said cheerfully. "I'm sorry I wasn't here to return your call. I was given the ultimate pleasure of viewing bureaucratic red tape in its purest form. I had an audience with the city's Commissioner of Mental Health."

"I'm certain you charmed him into eating out of your hand," Zachary said in a teasing tone.

Nicole's laugh was low and sensual. "I'm afraid any charm I possess was lost on the commissioner. He is a *she.*"

Then, she must have been green with envy when she saw you, he thought. "If she wasn't charmed, then she had to be impressed," he said instead.

"We'll know that once the city council goes over our budget."

"I'd like to meet with you to go over what I want when you evaluate your students," he said, deciding to eliminate any further mundane chatter.

"It can't be today, Zachary. My desk is covered with correspondence I must complete before..."

"Lunch, Nicole," he interrupted. "Give me an hour," he demanded quietly.

"Okay," she conceded. "But no more than one hour. Where do you want me to meet you?"

"I'll have a driver pick you up at twelve-thirty."

"I'll be ready," came her reply.

Zachary dialed his secretary's extension. "I want you to order lunch in for two. Then I want you to reserve a car to pick up Miss Nicole Moore from the East Harlem Family Services Center for twelve-thirty."

Knowing his instructions would be followed to the letter, Zachary returned to the drafting table set up by the wall-to-floor windows. He sat down on the high stool and began making notations on a pad as an undefinable feeling of confidence gripped him. A confidence that made him feel invincible.

Zachary's secretary met Nicole when the driver escorted her to the front door of Regan and Associates. She was an attractive young woman with curling black hair and dark eyes that were enhanced by her olive coloring.

"I'm Lisa Acosta," she said with a warm smile. "Mr. Regan is waiting for you."

Nicole wasn't given the opportunity to survey the tasteful furnishings in the reception area of the townhouse structure when Lisa led her down a narrow carpeted hall to an elevator. Plush carpeting in an electric blue lined the floors and the curving stairs leading to the upper floors of the three-story building. The electric blue carpeting was repeated on the floor of the elevator, but ended abruptly when the brass doors opened at the third floor.

Here highly-polished golden oak flooring took over. Nicole didn't know what surprised her more: the tall man wearing jeans, boots, a white wool turtleneck and a black and white pony-skin vest leaning against a desk, or the opulent furnishings in the office of the same man who had lent his name to his company.

Lisa stared at her boss, noting an expression she had never seen before. It was obvious that Zachary Regan was pleased to see Miss Moore.

"Will there be anything else, Mr. Regan?"

"No. And thank you, Lisa." He had spoken to his secretary but his eyes were trained on Nicole. A cream-colored mohair wrap coat hung open, revealing a slim olive green calf-length suede skirt and matching bolero jacket over a gold silk blouse. Saddle-brown low-heeled leather boots pulled her winning look together.

Zachary's long legs took him quickly across the room to her side as she shrugged out of her coat. He took it from her, folding it over his arm.

"The next time you come, I'll give you a tour of the building. There will be a next time," he added when she raised delicately arched eyebrows.

Nicole smiled, shaking her head. "Now I know why you and Adam are friends. Both of you have inflated egos."

His eyes crinkled behind his glasses. "It's called confidence."

Nicole tilted her head, looking up at him from under her lashes. Zachary's smile disappeared as he sucked in his breath. Her seductive gaze made him hot. And even if he'd stripped naked, he still would be burning.

"I'd say it's more like being swell-headed," she countered with a soft drawl.

Zachary flashed a mouth filled with straight white teeth, giving her his dimpled grin. "What do you expect from Howard men?"

"Not much, considering they're second-rate to the Morehouse brothers."

He hung her coat in a closet concealed within the wood paneled walls. "Spelman sisters and Morehouse brothers. What a sorry combination."

"Don't ever let my mother and father hear you say that. They met as students at Morehouse and Spelman."

Zachary caught Nicole's elbow and led her over to a table set up for dining near the windows. "I remember Adam saying that your father was quite put out because he selected Howard over Morehouse."

"I remember Daddy and Adam screaming at each other, but Adam wouldn't change his mind. My brother has a stubborn streak a mile wide." *As witnessed by his refusal to marry until after he's elected to a public office,* she thought.

Zachary seated Nicole at the large oval table set with translucent china, silver and fragile crystal on a royal blue linen tablecloth.

"We all have our own peculiar personality traits," Zachary remarked, taking his own seat opposite her. "Correct me if I'm wrong, Dr. Moore."

Nicole met his steady gaze across the table. "Why so formal, Zachary?"

"You are Dr. Moore, aren't you?" He spread a matching blue napkin over his lap, while watching the slight frown form between Nicole's eyes.

With the bright sunlight pouring through the windows, he noted Nicole and Adam shared the same tawny-brown coloring and large expressive eyes. Wherein Adam's were a dark green, Nicole's were a clear light brown. That's where the similarity ended. Adam's face was strong and masculine, while Nicole's was soft, delicate and undeniably feminine.

"I'm only referred to as Dr. Moore at the center," she informed him in a cool tone. She had completed a doctoral program at thirty, and received all of the honors conferred for a doctor of social welfare.

She unfolded her own napkin. "Does your secretary usually address you as Mr. Regan?"

"Not when we're alone."

"Do you insist she call you Mr. Regan in front of clients?"

"No."

Nicole's delicate jaw hardened. "Then I insist you not refer to me as Dr. Moore."

His mouth twisted in a wry smile. "I think it's odd that you don't acknowledge a title I'm certain you worked very hard to obtain."

She felt a prickle of annoyance. Zachary's teasing reminded her of a man she thought she'd been in love with who had referred to her as *Dr. Moore* whenever they disagreed on a subject; a man she wanted to forget.

"No more odd that you continue to wear a wedding ring even though you're a single man," she shot back in a soft voice laced with censure.

Zachary's expression stilled and grew serious as his black eyes flickered like burning coals. He stared down at his right hand as if seeing it for the first time.

"It's a matter of personal choice that I don't take it off."

Nicole looked at his lowered head, noting the tightly curling gray in the thick black strands. "And it's a matter of personal choice that I ask you not to refer to me as Dr. Moore," she retorted.

Zachary's head came up slowly. "Then it's settled, isn't it?"

Nicole was pulled into the heat of his burning gaze. For a brief moment a shimmer of knowing who they were and what they wanted from each other flowed between them: respect.

"Yes, Zachary. It's settled," she replied quietly. "I've promised you an hour, so I'd like to hear what you want."

Zachary pushed back from the table and walked over to his desk. Nicole's gaze followed him, visually examining the way his jeans hugged his lean hips and solid thighs. Why did he have to be attractive, she groaned inwardly. Why was his body so perfect? His casual attire outlined a well-conditioned physique that was still hard despite his sedentary work.

He returned to the table and placed a delicate full-leaded crystal and sterling silver hourglass in front of her. He gave her a perceptible nod, then turned it over.

"Your hour begins now, and you should consider yourself lucky that I'm not going to charge you for travel time."

The tense mood was over. He was back to teasing her. "I work for a non-profit organization," she replied, smiling.

"I won't bill your center, Nicole. I'd much rather bill *you* for personal services."

Her eyes widened. "How?"

Zachary retook his seat and uncovered several dishes. His eyes bathed her in admiration. "I've been invited to a formal dinner party and I need a date. You would be perfect."

He had said it so matter-of-factly that Nicole did not respond until she repeated his proposition to herself. She could not believe that Zachary Regan lacked for female companionship.

"I'm certain you know other women who would be more than willing to accept your invitation."

He shrugged a broad shoulder. "I'm sure they would," he replied without a hint of arrogance, "but they'd probably want a commitment or further involvement. With you there's no risk of that."

Nicole felt the heat rise in her face. Zachary saw her only as a pretty face; someone he could date, then walk away from; there was no way she could see him socially and not be affected by him.

"Does it matter that I'm seeing someone at this time?" If she had to she would use Carson as a shield."

Zachary began filling a plate with baked chicken and a rice pilaf. "Are you engaged to this *person?*"

"No."

"Then he shouldn't mind if I borrow his girlfriend for one night." He handed her the plate, registering the myriad of emotions crossing her face. "I told you before, Nicole, you're safe with me. I'm really rather harmless."

Zachary Regan was anything but harmless. He oozed lethal virility.

"It's the least you can do for me," he continued, filling a plate for himself. "I'm willing to give up my time to train a couple of students, in addition to offering them an adequate stipend." He shook his head and sucked his teeth. "Talk about being ungrateful..."

"Enough, Zachary," Nicole interrupted, laughing at his dour expression. "You've made your point." He picked up a bottle of wine, but Nicole covered her glass with the palm of her hand. "None for me, please. I have to go back to the office."

Zachary recorked the bottle and reached for a bottle of mineral water. He filled both of their glasses with the water. A satisfied smile tilted the corners of his mouth.

"So, you do have a conscience."

"No. It's just that you know how to heap on the guilt. You're a despot, Zachary Regan."

"I've been called worse," he remarked softly.

"I bet you have."

"You can call me anything you want, but don't make any plans for February first."

"What's happening on February first?"

"This dinner party given by close friends of mine will serve as a reception to show off their new house."

Nicole picked up her fork. "Did you design it?"

"I had some input." He glanced at the sand filling up the bottom of the hourglass. His hour with Nicole would soon be over. "I'm waiting, Nicole."

"Waiting for what?"

"For your answer. Will you be my date?"

"I have to check my calendar," she said.

Zachary seemed to accept her explanation as an affirmative when he nodded, then quickly outlined what she should look for in selecting a student for his company.

By the time the sand had filtered through the glass she was made aware of the differences between an architect, urban planner, engineer and interior designer. Zachary emphasized the general guidelines on curriculum in a typical school of architecture with varying programs offering a five-year course leading to a Bachelor of Architecture, while a few offered a Bachelor of Science in Architecture after six years of formal courses alternating with cooperative periods of work in the professional field.

"I'd recommend you consider the selection of a sophomore or a junior rather than a senior," he concluded. "An additional year of on-the-job training will give the student that extra edge when he or she applies to college."

Nicole nodded. She pointed to his drafting table. "What are you working on?"

He shifted his eyebrows in surprise. He thought she was only interested in placing her students. "Do you really want to see it?"

She laid aside her fork and reached out to turn over the hourglass. "Yes."

Zachary stood up and circled the table. Standing behind her chair, his gaze lingered on her hair neatly tucked into a French braid and pinned low on her nape. He wanted to undo her hair, thread his fingers through it and spread it out over her shoulders.

He wanted Nicole Moore. The realization stunned him. He wanted her in a way that he'd never wanted Julie; and anger, guilt and frustration assailed him.

His fingers curled around her upper arm as he helped her to her feet. Her shoulder brushed his chest, and when she turned suddenly her breasts replaced her shoulder against his chest.

Zachary was rooted to the spot, unable to move, breath. He watched the sweep of her lashes touch her cheekbones as she placed a trembling hand over his thudding heart.

Nicole looked up and her own heart lurched wildly. He was close, too close, and she felt the heat from his body flame and spread to hers when she detected a flicker of desire in the obsidian eyes.

"Nikki."

She shivered when he said her name. "Show me the drawing, Zachary," she demanded between clenched teeth.

He loosened his grip on her arm and directed her across the room and Nicole felt as if she was groping through a haze of unobtainable desire. Zachary had set the rules; he was forbidden fruit. But why did she feel as if she was being tested and tempted by his very presence?

She gathered her resolve and made a secret promise. After she placed her students with him, fulfilled her obligation for February first, she would not see Zachary Regan again.

Chapter Three

Nicole sat down on the stool, while Zachary stood beside her. She studied the intricate lines and curves he'd drawn on the blueprint sheet. It was only a drawing but she recognized its beauty immediately. She was so absorbed in the plans that she didn't see the pride in his eyes.

"I just completed it this morning," he said close to her ear.

"It's exquisite." Her gaze moved slowly over the large sheet spread out on the drawing board. "Hunter Manor," she read aloud. Zachary's neat print at the lower right hand corner identified the magnificent English Tudor structure.

"How long did it take for you to complete this?"

Zachary smiled down at her when she glanced up at him. "Ten months."

She shifted her eyebrows. "Does it usually take that long to design a house?"

"No. It always goes a lot faster when its a group project. But this one was a personal commission." His gaze went from her face to the intricate markings of Hunter Manor. "This structure is different from most others in that it is to be structurally engineered from the foundation through the framing. The architectural style is a blending of early English Tudor, with a noticeable influence of Louis XV and classic Country French. The interiors will be twentieth-century American. Eclectic styles, but quite interesting."

"How many floors?"

"Three. All of the main living areas will be located on the first floor. Each room will feature twelve-foot ceilings and oak wood floors in oversized herringbone patterns. The living room floor will have a Marie Antoinette design and will be hand-scraped for an antique appearance."

Zachary reached for a large book on a wood and brass table. He patiently identified and explained the architectural styles from different periods and Nicole was transfixed with the materials to be selected to make up the opulence of Hunter Manor: a nineteenth-century bricked archway and porte cochere, seven-and-a-half foot brick walls, a solid iron, electronically controlled front gate and specially carved limestone panels, slate roof, copper gutters and venting.

"The driveway and motor court will be of authentic Pennsylvania green stone," Zachary continued. "With more than twelve thousand square feet, the developer wanted it designed with a bent for entertaining. The foyer sets the tone with an elegant, sweeping staircase." He pointed to the entranceway and foyer.

"The staircase will be custom built with hand-carved newel posts, balusters and hand rails. During the daytime, the marble floor will glisten with streams of natural light from this window, and at night an antique light fixture will glow like a jewel on the marble floor."

"It's a bit rich for my taste," Nicole mused aloud.

"And for mine," Zachary concurred. "Thirty rooms, including five bedrooms, seven baths, three half-baths, a third-floor playroom and private servants' quarters, along with a five million dollar price tag is not quite within my means."

They shared a smile. "But for a work of art it is well worth it, Zachary." He turned back to the drawing, visually tracing his creation. "Why did you decide to become an architect?" she asked.

He didn't look up. "I never wanted to be anything else. I used to go to downtown Chicago and stand in the middle of the street and stare up at the skyscrapers and tell myself that I could've done this one better, or that one differently. I made a deal with my aunt once I entered junior high school: straight A's for art lessons."

"You've chosen a profession that permits you to embrace immortality. The architect-builders of the pyramids built their tombs to protect the deceased in their journey through eternal life, and you do the same for the living."

"I've never thought of my work in that way. I think of architecture as a way of shaping the physical environment so that it harmonizes with the aspirations of humanity."

"And you have succeeded," Nicole replied softly.

"But the gift you give humanity is a great deal more precious than mine, Nicole. You give of yourself; you're responsible for touching and shaping lives." He gave her a long, penetrating look. "Do you realize how special that can be? How special you are?"

Everything that wasn't Zachary Regan dissipated, leaving Nicole naked and vulnerable before a man who didn't want her. His eyes were black, blacker and more brilliant than polished onyx, pulling her into him and filling her with sensual anticipation she had never known. He came closer without moving and at that moment Nicole wanted to run and escape his awesome, magnetic powerful presence.

His right hand came up in a hypnotic motion, his fingers grazing the silken flesh of her jaw. "Do you, Nikki?" he questioned hoarsely.

"Yes, Zachary," she replied, her voice dropping another octave. "Yes, I know."

Reaching up, she pulled his fingers away from her face. "You can tell your driver to take me back."

He stared at her, unblinking. "I'll take you back."

"That won't be necessary, Zachary," Nicole protested. "I've taken up enough of your time."

"Today is a travel day for me," he informed her. "I'm scheduled to spend the weekend in Houston. A Texas developer has waited a long time for this design."

Nicole crossed her arms under her breasts. "Now, that's what I call perfect timing. Spending a weekend in the city that's hosting the Super Bowl."

He pursed his lips. "I hadn't planned it that way, but I'll take it."

"Don't forget to root for the *right team.*"

"And just who is the *right team,* Nicole?"

"Why the Jets, of course."

He grunted. "You've got to be kiddin'. Why should I root for losers? The Bears are going to annihilate the Jets."

"You're a traitor, Zachary Regan. You live in New York, yet you're going to support an out of town team."

He gave her a wide smile. "But my heart is still in Chica-go," he drawled in a midwest twang. "Give me another minute, then I'll drive you back."

Zachary returned to his desk and picked up the phone, giving Lisa a list of things he wanted her to complete before he left for the airport.

Nicole took the time to examine Zachary's office.

Washed by sunlight, the space combined ornate architectural detail with the best of a modern design. The blues,
beiges and tomato reds animated the detailed carved
paneled walls and plasterwork ceiling. The intricately
designed ceiling served as the massive room's centerpiece.

Two love seats in pale blue and a wingback armchair
in a darker blue and an oak coffee table were positioned on
a beige and blue patterned area rug in front of a fireplace.
Meticulously placed recessed lighting, integrated into the
plasterwork design, cast a warm glow on all of the highly-
polished wood surfaces and fired the brass sides of
Zachary's marble-topped desk.

Looking around, Nicole noticed the absence of art-
work and sculpture. There wasn't even a photograph of his
children. No pictures, diplomas or awards. The room
revealed a lot about Zachary Regan: he was a very private
person.

Zachary finished his call and hung up. He retrieved her
coat from the closet, helping her into it. He slipped a worn
black suede jacket over his vest, then punched the button
for the elevator.

"I'll be back in New York late Monday evening. I'll
be available for interviews from Tuesday on."

"I doubt whether you'll see anyone next week," Nicole
informed him. She had to wait for the parents of the
students to sign a release so that Vera could forward her the
data she needed to evaluate their children.

Zachary shrugged his shoulders in a gesture that
Nicole had come to recognize. "Whenever you're ready."

He didn't mind waiting. It meant that he would see
Nicole beyond their February first date.

He hadn't lied to her. There were a few women he
could ask to attend the dinner party with him, but none of

them had her poise. And he'd found Nicole enchanting, confident and spoiled; spoiled and secure enough not to be put off by his declaration that he did not want to remarry.

Her disclosure that she was seeing another man was what he needed to keep his emotions in check. That was something he'd learned as an adolescent--never encroach on another man's territory.

The elevator took them to the first floor and Zachary nodded to the receptionist as they left the building. He settled Nicole into the Mercedes parked across the street from the townhouse.

"How are you going to spend Super Bowl Sunday?" he asked after he'd pulled out into traffic.

"My boyfriend and I are throwing a party," she replied.

His right eyebrow rose a fraction. "That sounds like fun."

Nicole searched his impassive expression for a sign of guile. "It will be."

They did not exchange another word until he parked in front of the one-story brick structure housing the East Harlem Family Services Center.

Nicole studied his strong profile as he stared through the windshield. "Have a safe trip, Zachary."

His head came around slowly and he stared at her. She undid her seat belt and searched for the lever to unlock her door. Zachary released his own belt, then leaned over and captured her hand.

"Give me something to come back to," he said in a low, composed voice.

Nicole started, trying to comprehend what she was hearing. She was tormented by confusing emotions. Why was he giving her double messages? Sending her mixed signals?

"No, Zachary." Her answer was firm, final.

He leaned closer, his warm breath floating across her mouth. "Yes, Nikki," he moaned before his mouth covered hers. Her hands curled into fists, pushing against his shoulders.

"No," she gasped, opening her mouth.

It was what he needed for total possession. She trembled with the raw passion taking her to another level as his lips moved leisurely over hers in a light, nibbling action.

It was over as soon as it had begun. He smiled down at the apparent shock on her face. "Don't look so frightened, Nikki. It was only a little kiss."

This time when she pushed against the door he didn't try to stop her. She held her head erect and walked with stiff dignity to the center's entrance. She didn't dare turn around to see if he was still watching her.

Zachary stared at Nicole until she disappeared from sight. It was then that he lowered his forehead, resting it on his hands gripping the steering wheel. What the hell was he doing?

Nicole Moore was like an opiate; she was alluring and addictive; and he knew he was hooked the instant he'd tasted her honeyed lips.

He thought of his trip as a blessing. Spending time away from New York was what he needed to purge his mind of Nicole. He could forget her by immersing himself in work, but he wasn't certain that his body would let him forget. The ache in his loins was real; too real to ignore.

And for the first time in his life Zachary Regan felt as if he was losing control. Even after Julie had died, leaving him alone with three small children he had been in control.

He swore under his breath, the curses raw and ugly. He cursed Adam for introducing him to his sister, he cursed Nicole for her beauty and he cursed himself for letting her get to him.

Something within her called out to him—to get to know her; take the risk and become involved. But he couldn't take that chance. There was no way he could surrender his love to another woman. Every woman he'd ever loved died, leaving him empty and lonely. First his mother, then Julie. He could not repeat that with Nicole. No matter how much he wanted her, he refused to test fate.

"I'm back," Nicole announced to the receptionist after she had closed the front door with a resounding slam. "Hold all of my calls."

"Including emergencies?"

Nicole gave Cynthia Robinson a narrowed glare. "I'm not expecting any emergencies, Cynthia."

Cynthia's braided hair swung around her dark angular face. "But what if there are emergencies?"

Nicole let out an exasperated sigh. "Give them to Joe or Irene."

"Give what to me?"

Nicole headed towards her office, Irene Williams in pursuit. "Any emergency calls." She walked into her office and hung up her coat on the hook on the back of the door.

Irene flopped down on the chair beside a desk littered with paper. Shifting, she stared back at Nicole. "Are you all right?"

"I'm fine. Just fine." Nicole adjusted her jacket and made her way across the small space that she regarded as her second home. There were times when she spent more hours at the center than she did at home.

"Why the attitude, Nicole?"

Nicole sat down, not looking at the head psychologist. "Go away, Irene. I have work to do."

Irene tapped the hammered silver shields hanging from her lobes. A short natural hairdo, cat-like slanting eyes and a clear pecan-brown complexion afforded Irene Williams her exotic appearance.

"Would the *mucho* fine brother sitting outside in the Mercedes have anything to do with your less than friendly mood?"

Nicole's head jerked up. Very few things escaped Irene's all knowing eyes, and nothing was sacred at the center.

"Yes, Nicole. I just happened to be looking out of my office window when I saw who I recognized as E.H.F.S.C.'s genteel associate director in a tight clench with a man who I'm certain is as gorgeous below his shoulders as he is from his neck up."

"And I like the glasses, Nicole," Irene continued. "They make him look very scholarly. What does he do for a living that can afford him that cute little car?"

Nicole had to laugh. Irene was the only one she knew who could talk for a full minute before taking a breath.

"He's an architect."

"Hmm-mm," Irene crooned. "I've never met an architect. What's his name?"

If she didn't tell Irene, she would haunt her. "Zachary."

"And I've never met a Zachary. Not bad, Nicole. What's his last name?"

"Regan."

"Very different," she mused. "Like the former President?"

"No," Nicole corrected. "He was Reagan."

"One more question, then I'll disappear. Where does

he live? Is he married?''

"That was two."

"Please, Nicole," Irene pleaded.

"He lives on Long Island, and no he isn't married. He has three children, but he doesn't want to get married."

Irene scowled, shaking her head. "Now, someone ought to talk to that brother. Sleeping around is one thing, but making babies and not marrying your children's mother is something I don't approve of."

"He's a widower," Nicole said softly.

"I take back what I said about his being fine. No man is *that* fine if he's going to drop babies here and..."

"He's a widower," Nicole repeated. "His wife is dead."

Irene stopped her tirade, her jaw dropping. "Oh, no. The poor, fine brother" she crooned.

"Out, Irene," Nicole urged, smiling. "I have work to do."

"I'm going," Irene said. She left the chair and walked out of the office, closing the door behind her.

Someone should talk to Zachary, Nicole thought. He didn't know what he wanted--or did he? Was he using his widowed status as a device not to commit himself to any woman while he set out to seduce them?

Leaning against the back of her chair, Nicole caught her lower lip between her teeth. Well, if Mr. Zachary Regan was into playing games he was about to meet a master player. She had sparred with the best of them and always came up a winner.

Nicole picked up a monthly report that she had to complete and forward to the State's Department of Mental Health. It was nearly six-thirty when Joe Nash, E.H.F.S.C.'s executive director, came into her office, soliciting her input on administrative and bureaucratic changes. And when they finally left two hours later, Nicole was too wound up and too exhausted to think about Zachary Regan.

It was only after she'd completed her nightly ritual and lay in bed did the memory of his tender kiss sweep over her.

It was only a little kiss. That it was; but it was enough to denote the wild passion she was certain Zachary was capable of exhibiting.

* * * * * * * * * *

A loud groan went up from the people crowded into Carson Bates' SoHo loft apartment. The halftime score was Bears 24, Jets 3.

Nicole covered her face with her hands. The Bears were destroying the Jets.

Carson dropped an arm around her shoulders, pulling her sagging body to his chest. "Don't give up, darling."

Nicole lowered her hands and stared at Carson. "What happened to our defense?" she moaned.

"Defense! Defense!" chanted the more than two dozen people sitting on chairs, sofas and the floor.

Carson kissed her forehead, the coarse hair on his face scratching her tender skin. Carson had compensated for his thinning hair by affecting a short, neat beard.

"Do you want another beer, Nicole?"

"I just want to go home and cry," she replied.

"I'll take another beer, C.B.," shouted a male voice near the fifty-inch television screen.

"Get it yourself," Carson retorted. "I don't serve men."

"Don't ever get sick and come to Bellevue Hospital, Dr. Bates," warned the deep male voice.

"The same goes for you, Dr. Haywood, if you're up in my neighborhood. I haven't learned to distinguish an appendix from a heart," Carson shot back.

The room erupted in laughter, dispelling the pall of the Jets low score.

Nicole wound her fingers through Carson's, giving him a gentle smile. She had come to like the cardiologist. He was outgoing and sensitive, and she considered herself fortunate to call him friend.

She lay down on the thick white rug and cradled her head on folded arms. Staring up at the ceiling, Nicole closed her eyes. *Traitor,* she thought. *The traitor is probably delirious with joy. I'll pull his heart out of his chest if he says anything to me about the game.*

"What are you smiling about, Nick?"

Nicole reopened her eyes and stared up at Vera. Vera's short, naturally curling hair and rounded face always reminded her of the dolls she had when she was a little girl. And Vera Walker was doll-like with her cocoa-brown skin, large dark eyes and pert nose and mouth.

"I wasn't smiling. I was grimacing."

"Rough game."

"Tell me about it," Nicole sighed. "Perhaps we'll have better luck with the second half."

"I wouldn't count on it."

Vera was right. The second half proved as disastrous as the first, the game ending with a score of Bears 38, Jets 10.

Everyone was silent and depressed as they pulled coats from the closets and thanked Carson for his generous hospitality.

The somber mood continued when Carson drove Nicole back to her apartment. He saw her to her door, giving her a chaste kiss on her lips.

"I'll call you," he promised.

Nicole nodded and locked the door. She pressed her

fingers to her lips, comparing Carson's kiss to Zachary's. The pressure had been the same, but the intent wasn't. Zachary had held back. She couldn't stop herself from wondering what it would be like to experience the full rein of Zachary Regan's passion. *Just once,* she thought. *Just one time.*

Nicole had just completed signing the social work interns' quarterly evaluations when she heard a knock on her door. Glancing up, she saw the receptionist holding a large, gaily wrapped box.

"Who's birthday is it, Cynthia?"

"No one's. Your name is on the tag."

She rose slowly to her feet as Cynthia walked into the office. "Who's it from?"

"I don't know, Dr. Moore. Maybe there's a card in the box."

Nicole took the large package from Cynthia, shaking it gently. It was very light. She slid the red velvet bow off the box, then gently peeled away the silver-foil paper.

"Oh, how cute," Cynthia exclaimed when Nicole removed the cover.

"He didn't," Nicole ground out between her teeth. The box contained a large snow-white bear with a red satin bow around its neck. She picked up the stuffed animal.

She found the small gift card at the bottom of the box. She recognized the precise, neat print: *From one winner to another - Zack.*

"Is there a name on the card, Dr. Moore?"

Nicole swallowed back a smile. "Yes. It's from a..."

"Zachary Regan," came a soft male voice with a

midwest drawl.

Nicole stared at the tall figure framing the doorway to her office. "I thought you wouldn't be back until..."

"Tonight," Zachary finished for her as he stepped into the room. "I changed my mind and flew in last night."

Cynthia slipped behind Zachary in the doorway, noting he was impeccably dressed in a dark suit, white shirt and a maroon tie. His black cashmere top coat hung elegantly from broad shoulders and ended several inches above his ankles.

"Have you had breakfast?" he asked Nicole, his gaze moving with a seductive slowness over her face and body.

Nicole glanced down at her watch. It was nearly eleven. "It's too late for breakfast."

"What about lunch?"

"I can't," she said. She was scheduled to meet with the social workers at one.

Zachary adjusted his glasses and cocked his head at an angle. "Dinner?"

Her arms tightened around the bear, her closed expression not revealing the dizzying currents racing through her body, and she couldn't deny the spark of anticipation of sharing dinner with him. "I'm sorry, Zachary. Not tonight." She was not going to be that easy, that available for him.

Cynthia peered around Zachary's back and stared at Nicole, not believing she could turn down the man's invitation. She registered her censuring glare and decided to leave before Dr. Moore reprimanded her for snooping.

Zachary nodded and crossed his arms over his chest. "When, Nicole?" he asked quietly.

"Tomorrow night," she replied quickly. "We'll have dinner at my apartment. Seven o'clock." It would be on her terms or not at all.

This wrung a smile from him. "Red or white wine?"

She lifted her chin, returning his smile. "Bring both. I'm not certain what I'll prepare."

He gave her a mock bow. "Tomorrow at seven."

"Zachary?"

"Yes?"

She walked around her desk, stood in front of him and shoved the bear against his chest. "You traitor," she hissed, eyes narrowing.

"To the victor go the spoils," he whispered.

His hands shot out, capturing her shoulders. Only the stuffed animal prevented their bodies from touching. His head came down swiftly as he claimed her mouth in a hot, explosive kiss. This time there was no mistaking his passion when his tongue slipped between her parted lips.

He was like a starving man craving food as he searched the moist recesses of her sweet mouth. Raising his mouth from hers, he gazed into her eyes.

"Touchdown—Chicago," he rasped against her throbbing lips. He didn't give her a chance to reply when he spun around on his heel and walked out of the office.

Nicole squeezed the bear in a death grip. "I'll get you back, Zachary," she whispered softly. Her mind was working overtime when she returned to the desk.

Delicate fingers traced the plush material covering the bear's thickly-stuffed middle. *What are you,* she asked the bear silently, placing him on the desk in front of her. *Friend or foe,* she mused.

She examined the black button eyes and fuzzy nose. Picking up the bear, she pressed it to her chest. The scent of Zachary's after-shave lingered on the fur-like material.

He needed a name. A smile parted her swollen lips. Chicago! Yes, she would call him Chicago. And Chicago would be a friend.

And friends usually protected each other. She would need all of the protection she could muster if Zachary uncovered what she'd planned for him.

Chapter Four

"You are crazy, Nick," Vera gasped, watching Nicole examine her freshly-polished manicured nails. "You make an appointment to get your nails done, then ask me out for dinner when some man is waiting for you to eat with him."

Nicole blinked slowly. "Correction, Vera. He's waiting for me to *prepare* dinner for him," she replied in a bored tone.

"But you don't cook! You can make coffee—instant coffee--and you burn grilled cheese sandwiches. Anything beyond that makes you a natural disaster in the kitchen."

"He doesn't know that."

Vera's eyes grew rounder. "Why are you standing him up?"

A frown creased Nicole's smooth forehead. "Why? You ask me why, Vera Walker? Well, I'll tell you why. Because Zachary Regan is a little too sure of himself. He's the widowed father of three children who has no intention of remarrying. But the real joke is that he tells me he doesn't want to get involved, yet he's asked me out to breakfast, lunch *and* dinner," she enumerated, holding up a finger for each point. "He's even asked me to be his date for a formal dinner party.''

"I don't believe it," Vera said, laughing.

"Believe it. He says he's harmless."

"Is he harmless?"

"About as harmless as a cobra," Nicole managed to reply between stiff lips. "I'd prefer a rattler. At least he'd give a warning."

Vera leaned closer. "What did he do?" she asked, lowering her voice to a whisper.

Nicole picked up the small cup of brewed tea, taking a swallow. She watched Vera watching her. How could she tell her that even though Zachary had kissed her she wasn't repulsed by it?

Vera leaned back against the leather of the booth, her eyes crinkling in laughter. "The man got to you, didn't he, Nick? Your jaws are tight because for once you're not leading a man around by his nose. Zachary Regan sounds like he's his own person."

"I don't manipulate men, Vera."

Vera ignored Nicole's cold tone. "Do you like him, Nick?"

"What does liking have to do with an inflated ego?"

"Just answer the question. Do you like the man?"

What was there about him not to like, she thought. "Yes," she admitted after a lengthy silence.

"You like him even though he has three children?"

Nicole held up a hand. "Time out, Vera. What do his children have to do with me?"

"Only that you may have to consider whether you want to be a stepmother to his children."

"Vera," Nicole said, shaking her head. "You haven't heard a word I said. The man doesn't want to remarry. He doesn't want a stepmother for his children. He doesn't want to get involved."

"But he wants Nicole Moore."

"He doesn't want me," Nicole insisted.

"Then he wants to *see* you. And if he's invited you out for breakfast, lunch and dinner, then the man wants to *see* you."

"It sounds as if the both of you are fighting your feelings," Vera continued. "I see it all of the time with the kids at the high school. A boy likes a girl, but he insults her because he's afraid if he lets her know that he likes her she may reject him. It's a classic case of attack before you're attacked."

"Zack Regan is hardly a high school boy," Nicole mused aloud.

"But you're a woman, Nick. If you like the man, go after him."

"Are you suggesting that I go into a situation knowing that it's not going to go anywhere?"

"Are you looking to marry the man?"

"Of course not!"

Vera studied her thoughtfully for a moment, her expression skeptical. "What's different about this man?" she asked perceptively. "How do you know you can trust him?"

Nicole bit down on her lower lip, exhaling audibly. "I hope I can because he's Adam's friend.

Vera braced her elbows on the table and buried her face in her hands. "No! There can't be two of them in the world at the same time."

"Adam would've married you if you hadn't pushed him," Nicole said when Vera uncovered her face.

"I didn't push him, Nick. I merely mentioned that I was tired of waiting for him to make a commitment."

"He was committed to you."

"How often did I see him? Twice a month—if that

much.''

"Adam saw you when he could," Nicole explained, defending her brother. "When he couldn't come to New York he always sent for you to come to Virginia. The man spent a third of his salary commuting. Adam loved you, Vera. He loved you very much. But he won't tolerate anyone making demands on him.''

Vera's brown eyes grew misty. "And I still love him, Nick. I don't think I'll ever stop loving him." She sniffed loudly. "Talking about Adam doesn't solve your problem with this Zachary Regan.''

Nicole straightened her shoulders. "There's no problem, Vera.''

"Are you sure about that?''

Nicole tilted her dimpled chin. "As sure as you are about loving Adam.''

Vera sighed. "You're right about that.''

She smiled at her friend, nodding.

Nicole and Vera ordered dishes they had never sampled at their favorite Chinese restaurant, laughing about the men they'd dated when they shared the small one-bedroom apartment Vera still maintained.

Nicole glanced down at her watch. It was after ten. She smothered a laugh. "Do you think he's still waiting?''

"The poor man doesn't know how blessed he is, Nick'' Vera sputtered. "It's better that you stand him up rather than he eat your cooking.''

"Was my cooking that bad?''

Vera shifted her eyebrows. "Don't ask," she groaned. "That's why I cooked and you cleaned.''

Nicole waved away Vera's hand when she handed her a twenty dollar bill. "It's on me tonight. I'm more than willing to pay for the company.''

"What are you going to say to Zachary when he confronts you about not being home?"

Nicole wrinkled her nose. "I'll think of something."

She paid the bill and walked Vera back to her apartment building. Vera waited with her until she flagged down a cab.

"Let me know what he says," Vera said, hugging and kissing Nicole.

Nicole gave the driver her address, waving to Vera. Her outspread fingers curled into a tight fist when she thought about Zachary Regan. She hoped he'd learned his lesson. *She* would not be led around by the nose, *she* would not be a slave to his whims and he would learn that *she* could not turn her feelings on and off like a faucet.

Her luck ran out. She saw him leaning against a parking meter as she neared the corner, and a sigh of relief escaped her. Nicole wondered how long it would be before Zachary caught up with her; she had been avoiding him for days.

She had returned home and found his voice on her answering machine. Her number wasn't listed and no one at the center would've given out her home number, so she knew he'd probably called Adam. The following day she left strict orders with the receptionist not to put his calls through to her. It had continued until now.

Her gaze swept appreciably over his tall figure as he moved towards her. Today he had paired a dark brown leather duster with chocolate cords, a sand-colored pullover sweater and a pair of brown suede oxfords. Nicole wondered if he was dressed for traveling.

Zachary fell in step with Nicole as she walked down

Third Avenue. "Good afternoon."

She gave him a sidelong glance, smiling. "Good afternoon, Zachary. How have you been?"

His penetrating black eyes took in the curling ponytail flowing over her coat collar. "Well, thank you." He couldn't tell her the truth. He was angry—no, mad. Madder than he could remember ever being. Yet seeing her again somehow neutralized the rage he'd lived with since Tuesday night.

"I'm going for lunch," Nicole said evenly. "Would you like to join me?"

Her inviting him to eat with her flamed Zachary's temper. He caught her arm, spinning her around to face him. "No," he almost shouted. "What I'd like to do is wring your beautiful neck," he threatened in a softer tone.

Nicole's eyes widened in surprise. "What's the matter, Zachary?" She was hard-pressed not to laugh.

He tightened his hold on her arm. "You stand here, the picture of innocence, and ask me 'what's the matter?' I'll tell you what's the matter, *Dr. Moore.*"

"I told you not to call me that," she snapped.

Zachary's temper was past the breaking point. "I can't call you what I'd like to call you," he shot back. Leaning down, his face was mere inches from hers.

"This clown sweatin' you, Doc?"

They didn't see the man slip from the car parked alongside the curb. Nicole recognized the plainclothes police officer from a nearby precinct. He opened his short jacket, displaying a .38 in a holster under his arm.

Nicole saw the police officer's eyes narrow as he surveyed Zachary's face, then his hand on her upper arm.

"Everything's okay. My friend and I were just talking," Nicole explained. Zachary released her arm.

"No problem, Doc. As long as you were *talking.*"

Nicole looped her arm through Zachary's. "Are you joining me for lunch, or are you going to put on a show for the neighborhood? Remember, I live and work here."

Zachary walked along with Nicole until she turned into a coffee shop. A muscle throbbed noticeably in his jaw when she'd greeted and smiled at at least a half dozen people before they stepped into the warmth of the small restaurant. She greeted a waitress behind the counter in fluent Spanish, then pointed at a booth in the rear.

Zachary helped her out of her coat and hung it up with his on a row of hooks on a back wall. Nicole sat down, lacing her fingers together on the top of the table.

"Now we can talk," she said, surveying his impassive face when he sat down opposite her.

"Would he have shot me?"

"Who?" She knew who he was referring to.

"Your friend with the gun," he snarled.

"Officer Shelton? Of course not. He thought you were bothering me."

"The word was *sweating* you, Nicole," Zachary replied, still smarting from the cop calling him a clown. But the man hadn't been that far off. Where Nicole Moore was concerned he was a clown.

Nicole reached over and covered one of his hands with both of hers. "The people in this neighborhood are like family. We look out for one another. He was only trying to protect me."

Zachary felt some of his anger evaporating. He captured both of her hands between his, a thumb moving sensually over her smooth knuckles. His gaze was calm and speculative as it inched slowly over her face, taking in the rich color of her suntanned skin, the brilliant golden lights in her eyes and down to the full poutiness of her lush, succulent mouth; a mouth with a full lower lip he wanted to taste again and again.

His eyes swept over her hair, pulled back off her forehead and caught in a velvet ribbon. Her ponytail fell over one shoulder, curling over her left breast. It was the first time he had seen her hair without the confines of the tortoiseshell pins. He liked it.

Lowering his chin, he gave her a direct stare. "I'm going to ask you a few questions, and I'd appreciate honest answers." She nodded. "What happened to you Tuesday night?"

"I forgot about our date."

His fingers tightened on hers. "The truth, Nicole."

She closed her eyes. "I can't cook, Zachary."

He started laughing, the sound beginning in his chest and bubbling upward. "Why didn't you say that?"

Her lids flew up. "I burn grilled cheese. I burn toast. I..."

"That's all right, darling," Zachary crooned, seeing her pained expression. "I didn't ask you to cook for me."

Nicole felt her heart lurch when he called her darling. He was doing it again; he was playing with her.

"And I stood you up to teach you a lesson," she snapped recklessly.

His smile froze, his eyes narrowing behind his glasses. "You did what!"

Nicole pulled her hands out of his. She sat back, squaring her shoulders. "I stood you up," she admitted, tilting her chin.

"Why?" His jaw had tightened again.

"Because I'm a little tired of you playing games, Zachary Regan." She sat forward. "You tell me that you don't want to get involved and that I don't have to worry about..."

"I want to date you," he said, cutting her off.

Her mouth dropped open. "Stop playing with me," she warned heatedly, recovering quickly.

Zachary crossed his arms over his chest. "I'm not playing, Nicole." He heard her brief gasp of surprise. "I want to be able to call you up and ask you out to dinner without you thinking I'm after more than just your company. I'd like you to take in a concert or a play with me, go for long drives in the country and watch the seasons change and I want to go with you when you visit every antique shop in the tri-state area."

"Why?" It was her turn to question him.

He looked at her through half-closed lids. "Because I like you."

She turned her hands palms up and shrugged her shoulders. "That's it?"

He flashed a full grin, displaying white teeth and the sexy dimple in his right cheek. "That's it."

A warning voice went off in her head. Could she believe him? Did she really want to believe him?

It was simple, too simple. And because it was simple, she said, "All right, Zachary. I'll agree to see you when I'm not busy with other things."

A shadow of annoyance banished his grin. "Don't you mean *someone else*?"

A sudden chill hung between them with his question. "I had a life before I met you, and I'll have a life after you're gone," Nicole countered in an icy tone.

Nicole infuriated Zachary. She infuriated, frustrated and incensed him. And because he wanted to see her, he relented, saying, "Forgive me for being presumptuous."

She nodded. "You're forgiven."

Zachary felt the tightness leave his chest, the pain

subsiding. The knot had formed during the three hours he sat in his car with the two bottles of wine waiting for Nicole. She had put him through changes he had never gone through with any other woman.

He picked up the menu, not seeing any of the selections. A little voice in his head whispered that she was worth it. All he had to do was believe it.

"Where did you learn to speak Spanish?" he asked after they had given their order to the waitress.

"I perfected what I'd learned in high school when I spent my junior year of college in Spain."

"I was married in my junior year," Zachary replied in a reflective tone.

"Did you meet your wife at Howard?"

A momentary flicker of pain filled his eyes. "Yes."

"How did she die, Zachary?"

He couldn't hide the unspoken anguish when he closed his eyes. "She was involved in an accident with a drunk driver. It took her a week to die, while the driver of the other car walked away without a scratch."

"I'm sorry, Zachary." The words sounded so empty, but she had to say them.

He reopened his eyes, giving her a sad smile. "Thank you, Nikki."

The mood lightened when Nicole let Zachary sample the contents of her plate. She explained the differences in plantains as he chewed a piece of the fried banana.

"*Tostones de platano* are fried and sometimes served with crushed garlic in olive oil. The one you're eating is *maduro* or ripe."

Zachary swallowed, nodding. "I like it." He speared a forkful of rice and chicken. "What's this called."

"*Arroz con pollo*. Chicken with rice."

"This is good."

Nicole folded her hands on her hips. "You don't say. You've just about eaten all of it from me."

"Don't worry." He raised his hand to get the waitress's attention. "I'll order more."

Nicole looked at her watch. "Order it for yourself. I have to get back to the office. I work for a living, Zachary."

Zachary ignored his steak and picked up another forkful of chicken and rice from her plate. "So do I."

"But you own your company."

"Don't worry about it, Nikki. If you get fired I'll hire you."

"To do what?"

"I don't know. I'll create a position."

She laughed at his serious expression. "No thanks. I like what I'm doing."

They finished lunch and Zachary cradled the extra order of *arroz con pollo* under his arm as he walked Nicole back to the center.

"I have the data on six students. I'm setting up interviews with them for next week. I'll refer the ones I think would be best suited for you," she informed Zachary as they stood at the entrance.

"Good." He handed her the plastic bag with the food. "I ate your lunch, so you can have this for dinner." He gave her a sheepish grin.

She took the bag, realizing for the first time a boyish quality in his smile. It was easy, open and the dimple softened his face. "Thank you."

She turned to leave, but he caught her arm. "We have a date next Saturday. February first," he reminded her.

"What time should I be ready?"

"Cocktails are at seven, so I'll pick you up at six."

She glanced up at him through her lashes. "I'll be

ready."

"I'll be in touch," he returned softly, then turned and walked away.

Nicole didn't know why, but she wanted him to kiss her. She wanted a little something to remind her of him until they saw each other again.

Opening the door, she walked through the reception area. trying to make it to her office before she encountered Irene.

Irene met her halfway down the hall. "I think he looks like Herbie Hancock," she crooned as Nicole swept past her. "Does he have a brother?" she called out before Nicole closed the door to her office.

Nicole pressed her back against the door, experiencing a feeling of euphoria. It had worked. Standing him up had jolted him into reality.

And she would see him again. She would enjoy her time with him, and if it ended she still would have her memories.

"Yes," she whispered, closing her eyes. "Yes, yes, yes!"

Chapter Five

Zachary pulled his attention back to his chief architect's comments. His mind had been drifting all afternoon. When he least expected it his thoughts were of Nicole Moore. She had agreed to date him, easing some of his anxiety, but a foreign emotion, one he had not yet identified, continued to plague his waking moments.

He glanced around the conference table at the men and women who were responsible for the most innovative architectural designs to emerge within the last decade. Zachary considered them mavericks. They had combined their professional training, personal style, taste and convention to create the unexpected; and they were young and artsy enough to pull it all together to earn Regan and Associates numerous awards.

"Think about the populous," Zachary continued. "We're talking rural. They've existed with a main street running through the center of town for almost two hundred years. To them a large shopping mall will be seen as a large, imposing structure that's totally foreign to their environment."

"What do you recommend, Zack?" an engineer queried.

"A mall that looks like an enclosed main street. Gaslight-type street lamps, stained glass windows and brass handrails." He watched the flicker of excitement light up and widen the eyes of the half dozen people at the table. A mysterious smile tipped the corners of his mouth. "Try to work in some solar heating panels so that they conform to the overall greenhouse look of the design."

Lisa caught his attention when she stood in the doorway. "Well, gang, it's all yours."

"Aren't you going to work on this with us?" asked the engineer.

Zachary stood up, shaking his head. "Not this time. The developer is willing to pay for anything you come up with, and I give you my blessings."

There was an electrified babble as Zachary made his way out of the conference room. It was the first time they had been given license to design a project from beginning to end without his input. The design group had come a long way in the five years since they had begun working together as a team.

"Yes, Lisa?"

Lisa gave her boss a furtive glance. "Miss Moore is on the phone. She gave me the names of the students who are to be interviewed next week. She also said she's mailing the data you'll need on their coursework. I told her you'd probably want to talk to her. Is that all right?" she added in a reticent tone.

Zachary's grin gave Lisa her answer. "Of course it's all right."

Lisa watched Zachary's long legs cover the distance from the conference room to the curving flight of stairs leading to the third floor. Sometimes she didn't know why he had installed the elevator in the three story building, because he always walked up the stairs.

Zachary picked up the telephone in his office, sitting down on a corner of the desk. "Hello."

"Hello, Zachary. I hope I'm not interrupting you."

"Lisa knows to put you through whenever you call," he replied smoothly. "You'll never be an interruption, Nikki."

There was a pause before she spoke again. "I'm putting the information you'll need on your students in tonight's mail."

"Don't mail it. I'll pick it up."

"Don't bother, Zachary. I'll have someone drop it off to you."

"I'll pick it up *myself*, Nikki," he insisted. "What time are you getting off tonight?"

"I should be out of here by six-thirty."

"Are you going home?" he asked.

"Yes, but..."

"I'll come by your apartment and get it," he stated, cutting her off. "I'll be there at seven." He hung up, not giving her a chance to protest. "Checkmate, Nikki," he said softly.

Crossing his arms over his chest, Zachary stared out through the windows. The lengthening shadows heralded the approach of nightfall. It appeared as if his uneasiness was more apparent at night; and it was when he lay in bed alone that the emptiness was magnified. Six years; it was six long, lonely years since he had spent an entire night with a woman.

He ran a hand over his face. Maybe he was working too hard; maybe he was getting old; and maybe he needed to take a break. He would take a week off when the children were released from school for their winter recess, and they would spend time in Vermont skiing.

He thought about Nicole skiing and he shook his head. A smile smoothed out the vertical lines between his eyes. Nicole would never ski. She hated cold weather.

Nicole watched Zachary's approach as he made his way down the hall. His arms were filled with two brown paper bags. "What's that?" she asked as he brushed past her.

"Where's your kitchen?"

"To the right of the dining area." She closed the door and followed him into the small utility kitchen. He had put down the bags and was emptying their contents onto the countertops. "What are you doing, Zachary?"

He smiled at her. "I bought you some food."

She folded her hands on her hips. "I don't need food."

"It's dinner."

"For who?"

Zachary held up a bottle of red wine. "For us. And this bottle of wine has been waiting a long time for you," he crooned, giving her a direct look.

Nicole slipped her hands into the pockets of her jeans, pulling the fabric taut across her slim hips. She shifted her eyebrows, smiling. "Now, I understand. You're paying me back for standing you up."

"Not only are you beautiful, but you're also brilliant," he taunted.

Nicole stared at Zachary and some sixth sense made her aware of the Zachary Regan under his tasteful casual attire and glasses. He had not become the owner of a successful architectural firm at thirty-nine because of his talents. There was another facet to his personality that said he was strong, unyielding and unforgiving when he had to be. She had also glimpsed his controlled fury when she encountered him on the street when he'd waited for her. She had hoped to break him, bend his will, and teach him a lesson. However, Zachary was an excellent opponent.

She pulled a hand out of her pocket, extending it. "I can say that we're now even."

He stared down at her slender hand, then his gaze moved up to her mouth. "No more games, Nikki?"

Nicole smiled. "No more." He grasped her fingers, bringing them to his lips. A slight shudder wracked her when he turned her hand over in his and pressed a kiss to her palm.

"Good," he said softly. He released her hand and pulled his arms from a short wool jacket. "You can hang this up while I wash my hands and start dinner." He noticed her slight frown.

She gave him a disapproving glance from under her lashes. "What?"

"*Please,* Nicole."

She took the jacket, giving him a saccharine smile. "That's better."

"Spoiled wench," Zachary muttered under his breath as she turned and walked out of the kitchen.

He leaned against the counter, still seeing the seductive sway of her hips in the fitted jeans. Nicole was sexy without even trying.

She returned to the kitchen and stood next to him. Her warmth and smell were tantalizing. Raw desire made him want to crush her body to his, permitting her to feel the longing, the heat, as it raced headlong and uncontrollably throughout him.

"Where's your bathroom?" His voice was a bit gruff, but he couldn't help it. He wanted her. He wanted to make love to her. As soon as the thought entered his head, he banished it.

She was his friend's sister; he didn't want to become involved; he couldn't fall under her spell.

Excuses. They were all excuses. His brain said no, while his body telepathed yes.

He made it to the bathroom and closed the door. Moisture had formed on his upper lip. What the hell was happening to him? Even when he met Julie his desire for her was never that strong. He'd loved Julie, but she never inspired the swift and violent sensual reaction he was feeling with Nicole.

Zachary stared at his reflection in the mirror over the sink after he'd washed his hands and splashed cold water on his face.

He dried his face on a towel, looking around the bathroom. All of the fixtures in the pale green and rose-pink room were modern, but it ended there. Porcelain pots with decorative soaps and potpourri in a cloying lemon fragrance, lace-edged towels and crystal bottles filled with bath salts and lotions transported him back to an age of gracious and elegant living.

He replaced his glasses. Nicole Moore had been born too late. She belonged to America's gilded Victorian age where she'd lounge on a wicker love seat in a latticed gazebo, wield a delicate lace fan and sip iced tea, while a group of young suitors courted unsuccessfully. None of their silvery words or priceless gifts would be enough to turn her head. She would stare down her nose at them, then tilt her chin to catch whatever breeze would avail itself to cool her fevered face above the white high-neck dress. She would always be certain to have the wide hat with a trailing stream of veil on hand to protect her delicate skin from the angry rays of the summer sun.

But he would court her, and she would ask him back again; again and again until...

Zachary let his thoughts trail off. He usually did not indulge in daydreams.

He knew he'd been right when he saw that Nicole had set the table in the dining area. There was a setting for two with a lace tablecloth and delicate white china with handpainted lilacs. Linen napkins with lace edges were folded on each plate.

"Do you prefer candles or the artificial light?" she asked when she noticed him staring at the table.

"The candles will be nice if you don't draw the drapes."

Nicole reopened a massive bleached pine armoire that served as a china and linen closet and withdrew a pair of magnificent silver candlesticks. She completed the table with heavy silverware and crystal goblets.

"You set a beautiful table, yet you don't cook," he teased.

"I don't cook because I never learned to cook."

Zachary walked back to the kitchen. "Why not?"

Nicole followed him. "Because I was too busy playing ball or going fishing with Daddy. My mother used to complain, but Daddy said there were always restaurants, or I could hire someone to cook for me."

"Your father's right on that account. There're always the restaurants. Unless you have a cook hidden away somewhere around here."

Nicole slipped behind Zachary and wound her arms around his waist, pressing her breasts to his back. "No, I don't. But if you're good, I'll hire you," she whispered against his broad sweatered back.

Zachary went stiff. He dropped the potato he had been rinsing under the running water, his breath coming fast. "Nicole," he groaned painfully.

She released him and sat down on a tall stool, flexing her bare toes on the rung. "Okay, so you're a temperamental cook."

"How many men have cooked for you?" He couldn't look at her.

Nicole braced her elbows on her knees and supported her chin on her fists. "Not too many."

"How many is not too many?"

"One."

His head spun around. "One?"

She flashed a wide smile. "You." Her smile slipped away. "That makes you very special, Zachary Regan."

And he was special. But what he didn't know was how special he was becoming to her. She didn't know what made her hug him; she hadn't been able to stop herself.

She examined his strong wrists where he'd pushed up the sleeves to his sweater. Her gaze caught the band on his right hand and she closed her eyes. The ring was a constant reminder that Zachary was not free; a dead woman held his heart and she had not released him; not even in death.

"Let me put on some music, then I'll help you. I can wash lettuce and make up a salad," she stated when he gave her a skeptical look.

"So you do cook."

"A green salad does not require heat, wise guy."

She moved off the stool and walked into the living room. Two shelves in the built-in bookcase contained albums, cassettes and a compact disc collection. Nicole decided to put on a cassette with selections she had taped from a station that featured past as well as the latest hits.

Music flowed from the speakers as she turned off the lamp in the living room, leaving the space dark except for the burning tapers on the table and the silvered moonlight coming in through the expanse of wall-to-wall glass.

Zachary met her as she returned to the kitchen, capturing her arm and pulling her back into the living room.

"Dinner will have to wait until we dance to this one," he said close to her ear. "It's one of my favorites."

Nicole was swept into the circle of his embrace, one hand planted in the small of her back, the other gripping her fingers firmly. Closing her eyes, she permitted herself to float, glide, as the harmonizing voices of Roberta Flack and Donny Hathaway crooned in, *"The Closer I Get To You."*

Desires, longings, spirit and flesh fused, and Nicole didn't know where it began. All she knew was that the slender thread that had formed the first time she met Zachary tightened, binding her to him and she didn't want to escape. She was wrapped in an invisible warmth as it closed in on her. She didn't want to be free; she wanted Zachary to be her keeper; the keeper of her heart. She stumbled, missing a step, but his strong arm steadied her.

Burying her face in the hollow between his neck and shoulder, Nicole gave into the emotions she had been fighting for days, weeks. She knew her feelings for him had been intensifying, but she was helpless to fight it; and her feelings for him had nothing to do with logic or reason.

Her arms circled his waist as she pressed her cheek to his chest. She felt his chin rest on the top of her head. This made her smile. She hadn't known many men tall enough to do that. She sang along with Roberta when Zachary echoed Donny, both of his arms wrapped tightly around her midriff.

The song ended and they clung to one another, trembling with a need that they hadn't thought possible. Nicole raised her face in the darkness, trying to see his expression.

Her breasts rose and fell heavily under the cotton T-shirt. "Thank you, Zachary." Her voice was low, husky.

Zachary used his own method to demonstrate his appreciation. His mouth moved over hers, devouring its moist sweetness. His claim was slow and unhurried. He took nibbling bites of her lower lip, then the upper, teasing and frustrating her.

Her hands framed his face when she tried capturing his ravishing mouth. Long, strong fingers locked around her wrists, frustrating her further.

"Zachary!" His name came out in a sob.

His name on her lips shattered his fragile control. Easing her down to the carpeted floor, he covered her body with his.

"Zachary!" This time when she called out his name it was strident. She hadn't expected the dance to end with them coupling on her living room rug.

His lips brushed her brow. "I'm sorry, Nikki. I didn't mean for it to get out of hand," he apologized.

Her hands moved slowly over his damp flesh under the sweater. "It's all right, Zachary. It's all right," she repeated over and over.

He helped her to her feet and they returned to the kitchen. They were content to listen to the taped music as they moved cautiously around each other in the small space.

He's dangerous, Nicole thought, giving Zachary surreptitious glances. *And he's a heartbreaker*, she mused further. She, who had earned her living counseling others, needed someone to counsel her. She was falling for a man who refused to offer her the security of sharing his life or his future.

"How do you like your steak?" Zachary asked stiffly.

"Well," she replied, monosyllabic.

"Nicole."

"Zachary."

They had spoken in unison.

"You first," Zachary offered.

Nicole's shoulders dropped as she let out her breath. "I'm willing to forget what just happened if you can."

Zachary blinked at her, unable to believe she could dismiss the blatant passion that had passed between them. He knew she was a passionate woman, but he couldn't understand how she could turn off her emotions so easily.

"Consider it forgotten," he shot back.

Together they concocted a meal of warmed Italian bread, baked potatoes, broiled steaks and a green salad of torn romaine lettuce with a sprinkling of parmesan cheese with a vinaigrette dressing.

"You lied to me," Zachary accused softly, twirling a small amount of wine around in his glass. He'd removed his glasses, and the soft light glimmered in his black eyes.

"About what?" Nicole held her own glass out to be refilled.

"You said you couldn't cook." He poured a rich, dark-red burgundy into her glass.

"I can't. You baked the potatoes, broiled the steaks and mixed the salad dressing."

"The microwave oven did it, Nicole. You have the latest state of the art microwave-convection contraption and still you don't use it."

She stared down into the depths of the wine, seeing the reflection of the flickering candle flames. The golden glow was favorable to the delicate planes and hollows of her face.

"My intentions were good, Zachary. When I moved in I made all sorts of plans." Her head came up. "One plan was to learn to cook. I even bought a few cookbooks," she added, seeing his smile. "But then I became more and more involved in the work at the center. Our one late night a week soon became two and now three.

"We've become the lifeline between the residents and the other bureaucratic agencies. Without us, most of these people would not survive. Medicaid, supplemental food stamps, meals on wheels and home attendant services. Many people never think of these services until they need them.

"Then there's individual and family counseling. We help families cope with a drug-addicted son or daughter, or the increasing incidents of child abuse and domestic violence." She took a swallow of wine, her gaze fixed on his solemn face.

"After dealing with all of this and the bumbling idiots who sit in their plush offices and tell you that a family of four should be able to exist quite comfortably on ten grand a year, I can't think about learning to cook. Somehow that's not important, especially when there're thousands of people in this city who don't have anything to cook, even if they knew how."

A brittle smile parted her lips. "I'm sorry, Zachary. I didn't mean to lay all of this on you. When I get on a soapbox it's hard for me to get off."

"It's all right, sweetheart. I don't mind hearing it." He watched, transfixed, as her mouth softened. "Anytime you feel a need to unload, you can call me. My shoulders are broad enough to carry it."

That she had no doubt. His V-neck black sweater displayed his strong neck and a thick mat of curling chest hair. *He should be forced to wear a sign around his neck reading: "This man is a dangerous substance. Use with extreme caution,"* she thought.

The tortoiseshell Hermes clock on the desk chimed ten o'clock and Nicole observed Zachary from under lowered lids. He made no attempt to move. "Don't you think you should be getting home to your children?"

"Are you putting me out, Nikki?"

A rush of heat stole into her cheeks. "No. I just don't want to be responsible for keeping you away from home."

Zachary studied her face, as if he wanted to commit it to his memory. "I'm not going home tonight."

Nicole sucked in her breath. Zachary wasn't staying with her, so that meant he was going to see another woman. A lump tightened in the pit of her stomach when she thought about Zachary and another woman; a woman who would share his kiss and his body.

"I'm going back to the office." He didn't hear her exhale softly.

Nicole felt her heart racing with relief. "Aren't you going to sleep at all?"

"Probably not." He pushed back from the table. "I'll sleep when I get home."

"And when's that?"

"Tomorrow morning. I'm taking the next two days off. That's not going to sit too well with Kathy and the boys, but they don't have a choice."

"I take it they prefer not having Daddy around the house too much," Nicole said perceptively.

He stood up, nodding and smiling. "You've got that right. They've managed to get over on Henrietta and house rules have become somewhat relaxed lately. I must remind Davy and Danny that eating in their bedroom is prohibited, and Kathy's not to make or receive any phone calls after ten."

Nicole rose with him and began clearing the table. "They sound quite normal to me."

Zachary took the stack of plates from her hands. "I suppose they are, but parents always think of their kids as weird."

"You don't know what weird is until you've been a caseworker." She filled the sink with soapy water and began rinsing the dishes before loading the dishwasher. "There were times when I doubted whether some people are actually human beings."

Zachary registered the pained expression on her face. "You've seen it all, haven't you?"

She nodded. "Just about."

He moved closer and curved a hand around her waist. "Does it ever turn you off, or make you want to walk away from it all?"

Tilting her chin, Nicole saw that he wasn't making fun of her. "No Zachary. No, it doesn't."

His fingers played with the single plait falling down between her shoulder blades. "If you ever have a need to get away, escape, let me know."

She exulted in the comfort of his nearness as her eyes moved slowly over his lean, smooth, dark-brown face. "Where would I go?" she asked tremulously.

He took a step, his chest grazing her shoulder. "It's where would *we* go, Nikki. I'd take you away where you'd never have to worry about whether it's morning or night. I'd help you to relax and forget about the outside world and all of its weirdos. Even if you need a weekend, let me know. No strings attached," he added when her golden eyes widened.

"Thank you, Zachary," she whispered.

Leaning over, he dropped a light kiss on her parted lips. "You're welcome."

He helped her clean the kitchen, then prepared to leave. She stood at the door, watching him put on his jacket. "Thank you for dinner."

"Thank you for the company." He gave her a warm smile. "Don't forget we have a date for Saturday."

"I won't forget."

He kissed the tip of her nose, winking. "I'll be in touch."

Nicole locked the door and took a quick dance step across the entry. She floated into the living room and sank down on a love seat. She sat there listening to the taped music until it ended and the scented tapers burned out, leaving a fragrant scent of lemon spice in the darkened space. It was only then that she retreated to the bathroom to begin her nightly ritual before she went to sleep to forget about how Zachary Regan made her feel whenever they were together.

He didn't want to become involved and neither did she, but somehow their passions were ignoring everything their lips uttered.

Chapter Six

Nicole stood with her back to the floor-length mirror on the door in her bedroom. "Damn," she muttered angrily. She couldn't button all of the buttons along the back of her dress. She had worn the dress once before, but that was when she lived with Vera. There were definite drawbacks to living alone.

The dull buzz on the intercom indicated Zachary had arrived. Slipping her feet into a pair of black satin heels, Nicole rushed out of the bedroom.

"Yes," she answered through the intercom.

"Zack," came his mellow reply.

She pressed the button, releasing the downstairs door lock and waited, compressing her lips together. Two minutes later, Zachary walked through the door, his startled gaze mirroring his approval of her appearance.

Zachary did not believe Nicole could improve on perfection; but she had. She'd cut her hair, a fringe of bangs sweeping over her forehead, and a loose, swingy pageboy ending an inch above her shoulders. Large oval onyx studs, banded in gold, were inserted in her pierced lobes.

His gaze moved slowly down to her body. Her dress, a black silk crepe, was molded to her willow-slim form, emphasizing the flatness of her middle. The feature that captivated him most was the bodice and sleeves. They were made of black lace, and her golden brown flesh shimmered through the gossamer material. Artfully designed interlocking dragons crisscrossed her breasts, providing Nicole a measure of modesty and giving new meaning to a 'basic black dress'.

The bright red color on Nicole's mouth glistened seductively when she smiled. "I need your help." Turning, she presented him with her back. "I missed a few."

His fingers were clumsy, but he managed to fit the tiny lace-covered buttons in their fastenings. Nicole was not wearing a bra under the exquisitely seductive garment. Just knowing she was bare under the delicate material sent a spasm of uneasiness through him. Since meeting Nicole, Zachary had not thought about or sought out another woman, denying himself the physical release his body craved.

Leaning closer, he inhaled the tantalizing fragrance of her perfumed hair and body. "Will you need my help getting out of it, too?"

Nicole tried turning around, but his fingers had circled and tightened around her tiny waist, making her his prisoner. A warm, tingling shiver of wanting swept through her. She had seen Zachary five times, and each time it became more difficult to conceal her increasing desire for him.

"Probably," she responded in a dreamlike voice.

"You've surpassed perfection, Nikki," he crooned, his lips moving over her thick, luxurious hair. "You look wonderful."

His grip loosened and Nicole turned around. "Thank you," she replied, her gaze moving slowly over his face.

Zachary was resplendent in formal wear. A flowing black silk duster hung open, revealing a tuxedo with a pleated front shirt, onyx studs, a bow tie in a red, yellow and green kinte cloth and a matching cummerbund. He'd exchanged his gold wire-framed glasses for a pair in black.

"You're no slouch yourself, Zack Regan," she returned with an appreciative smile.

He nodded, silently acknowledging her compliment. His eyes glowed with an unnamed fire as he stared down at her smiling mouth. His expression was closed, revealing none of what he was feeling. Nicole would've been shocked if she could read his thoughts.

"I don't think I want to share you with anyone tonight," he stated quietly. "I want you all to myself."

Her mind floundered. He wanted her; he wanted her, yet he wasn't willing to offer her any assurances that she could and would be considered as an integral person in his life or future.

To Nicole, desire and wanting were the same. Zachary wanted her and she wanted him. But her desires went beyond a physical one. She wanted to be more than a willing receptacle for his lust; she wanted permanence, love and a commitment.

Commitment. The word even shocked her. Now she knew how Vera felt two years before when she sought a commitment from Adam.

"I didn't fight with the buttons on this dress to stay home tonight, Zachary Regan," she said haughtily.

He managed a tight smile. "Then, I guess that means we'd better get going."

Nicole grasped a dark, full-length fur coat thrown over the love seat and handed it to Zachary. He helped her into it, then picked up her small sequined evening purse, slipping it into the pocket of his duster.

They rode the elevator down to the lobby in complete silence, smiling at one another. She mimicked a silent wolf whistle and winked at him, and Zachary dissolved in a spasm of laughter as they walked out of the building, hand in hand.

The toes of the satin-covered heels peeked from under the hem of her dress and coat as Nicole walked briskly alongside Zachary. February had come in like a lion, the wind wild and biting.

"Six more weeks, Nikki," Zachary reminded her when she huddled closer to his body.

"I won't make it, Zachary," she exclaimed.

His right arm went around her waist, pulling her even closer to his side. "Yes, you will. This has been an unusually cold winter."

"I'd love to be a bear and sleep in all winter."

"You'd never make it," he teased. "You'd never eat enough to last you through your hibernation period. You pick at your food like a bird."

"That's because I'm used to eating on the run."

They arrived at his car. Bending over, Zachary unlocked it and helped her in. He circled the car and moved in beside her. He started up the engine, smiling at her. "Hang out with me and you'll eat like a ravenous beast."

"And you'll make me fat," she said with a slight pout. "Then you'll be forced to buy me a complete new wardrobe." She gave him a sidelong look. "I don't come cheap, Zachary."

Zachary shifted into gear, pulling away from the curb. "It would be cheaper to feed and clothe you than to set you up in a residence." He managed a quick glance at her delicate profile. "I have an idea how much you paid for your desk."

Her left hand caught his right on the steering wheel. "And I bet you can't wait to tell Adam."

Zachary shook his head. "No, Nicole. I wouldn't do that." Her hand fell away and he missed its warmth. "Adam and I are friends, but not close friends. He lived on campus, while I stayed in a rented room. We knew each other because we pledged for the same fraternity. By the third year we rarely saw one another. I was married, so I stopped hanging out with the single guys. Adam and I lost contact after graduation, and it was seventeen years before we met again.

"I was in D.C. on business when I ran into him on Connecticut Avenue. We had a few drinks and he told me about the house he had bought in Arlington. I extended my stay and went out to see it. The moment I saw the farmhouse, I visualized how it should've looked restored to its original state. Adam commissioned me to draw up the plans, and less than a year later it was habitable."

"Adam never mentioned your name to me. He only said that a fraternity brother had redesigned the house."

Zachary turned onto the street leading to the Triborough Bridge and Long Island. "And he never mentioned your name until I met him at the restaurant the night we met. I knew he had a younger sister but nothing beyond that. I suppose he was the big brother protecting his little sister."

Nicole affected a slight frown. "He wasn't that protective when he gave you my unlisted telephone number."

"Instinctively, he knew he could trust me with you."

"Why? Because you're *harmless?*"

Zachary's right hand searched under her coat and closed over a knee. "That I am, babe," he drawled in a lecherous voice."

She slapped his hand away, laughing. "You're sick."

"Sick how? Perverted sick?" He wiggled his eyebrows.

"Silly sick."

"Sometimes, Nikki. Only sometimes." His expression stilled and grew serious. "And only with you."

Nicole stared at the lighted dashboard rather than look at Zachary. *Only with her.* She was the exception. She was just that non-threatening to his future.

"Is that a compliment, Zachary?"

"What do you think?" he asked, concentrating on his driving.

"I don't think it is."

"Then you think wrong, Nicole."

Instead of buoying her spirits, his admission left her feeling flat, defeated. An inner torment began to gnaw at her. If she continued to see him she would be leaving herself open for heartbreak, and she was too much of a survivor to entertain that possibility.

Zachary could offer her his charming company and intellect, but nothing emotional beyond that.

He was physically attracted to her--she'd known that from their initial meeting, but he didn't need her physically. She was mature enough to know that Zachary Regan was not undergoing any sexual deprivation. He was too young, too virile, to remain celibate for long periods of time.

"What are you thinking about, Nikki?" His soft voice broke into her thoughts.

"You," she replied quietly.

"What about me?"

"About you and other women."

"What about me and other women?"

"Are you sleeping with someone?"

She caught him off guard. She certainly was honest and direct. But then Nicole Moore was a professional counselor.

"Not now," he answered as honestly as he could. And he wasn't. Not since he'd met her. "Why?"

Nicole shrugged a shoulder. "Just curious."

"My wife died, Nicole, and I don't think she wanted me to die with her."

"I'm certain she didn't."

"What if the scenario was reversed," Zachary began. "What if you were married and your husband died, leaving you with a child or children. Would you date again, or remarry?"

Nicole stared out through the window at the brilliant New York City skyline, millions of stars resembling a sprinkling of diamond dust on black velvet.

"It would depend on the man, Zachary. If I loved him enough I would marry him," she replied carefully.

"And you wouldn't feel as if you were being unfaithful to your late husband's memory?"

Her head came around and she stared at Zachary. "Of course not. Because whatever I'd shared with him could never be repeated with anyone else. Each man would be special to me; special and deserving of whatever love I had to offer."

"Sounds good," he said cynically.

"But you don't believe it, do you?" she countered, her temper rising.

"I don't know what to believe anymore," he admitted.

"Remarrying doesn't make one unfaithful, Zachary. Not even when a marriage ends in divorce. And it certainly wouldn't apply in the event of a death. You said your wife wanted you to go on living; and you should; not only for your children but also for yourself,'' Nicole added in the soft, gentle tone she used in counseling.

A muscle twitched uncontrollably in Zachary's jaw. ''What are you trying to say, Nicole?'' His voice was cold, accusatory.

''I *am* saying that you need someone other than your children. Someone with some permanence; a woman who wouldn't be available just for your physical needs. A woman you can laugh with. A woman *you* can love, and who'll love you in return.''

''I don't want to love another woman,'' he ground out between his teeth.

He felt rather than saw Nicole withdraw. She turned her head to the side window, staring as the towering structures of Manhattan's skyline faded behind them.

What he meant was that he was afraid to love again, even though a nagging inner voice taunted him relentlessly for years.

After Julie's death he had floundered emotionally, knowing he had to find someone to take care of his motherless children when his in-laws mounted a campaign to secure custody of their grandchildren. He had been left with two toddlers and a frightened little girl who'd doted on her mother and imitated her every move and nuance. Within one week a happy, secure family unit was splintered with tragedy; a tragedy that took the life of a young woman who was in love with her husband, children and life itself. He rebounded quickly, reassessed his priorities and set out to secure and protect his children.

He had succeeded. He'd taken all of the steps needed to provide Kathy, Danny and Davy with what they needed financially and emotionally, successfully establishing a truce with his mother and father-in-law; however it wasn't until he'd met Nicole Moore that Zachary realized he had taken care of everyone but himself.

His vow to not become involved with a woman had been shattered the moment he saw her. He may have mouthed the words but they were as empty as the wind. An even more terrifying realization was that he couldn't imagine not seeing her.

A quiet, natural silence filled the car when Zachary turned on the radio. Familiar landmarks and road signs blurred into a familiar pattern as he followed the parkway leading to Long Island. He traversed the same road every day, accelerating and decelerating by instinct. He didn't have to concentrate on the road. All of his senses were attuned to the tall, slender woman sitting beside him.

Nicole had glimpsed the sprawling properties along Long Island's north shore communities during the drive from Manhattan, but she still was not prepared for the magnificent brick and stone three-story structure situated on four acres of lush, verdant professionally landscaped grounds.

A young blond youth approached the car as Zachary maneuvered into the commanding circular drive.

"I'll park it for you, Mr. Regan." He didn't look old enough to drive.

"Thanks, Reno," Zachary returned, smiling.

Zachary shifted into park and came around the car to help Nicole. His grip tightened on her gloved hand when he pulled her gently to his side.

"What did you do to this one?" she asked, staring up at the sweeping nineteenth-century house.

Zachary gave her a mysterious smile as he led her up the four stone steps leading to the front entrance portico. "Not much."

Nicole did not have time to react to his "not much" when the door opened and a very pregnant blond woman greeted them. She recognized the resemblance between the woman and the young man Zachary had called Reno immediately.

"Bless you for coming, Zack," she sighed, stepping into his outstretched arms. "It just wouldn't seem right to open my home to guests and not have the man responsible for its grandeur present." She placed a light kiss on Zachary's smooth jaw.

His eyes crinkled in a smile. "I told you I wouldn't miss your grand opening." Releasing his hostess, he draped an arm around Nicole's waist. "This is Nicole Moore. Nicole, Janine Prescott."

Janine's topaz-blue eyes widened, taking in the tall woman beside Zachary. A pale eyebrow shifted slightly before a friendly smile parted her lips. "Hello, Nicole." Surprise lowered her voice to a throaty whisper.

"My pleasure, Janine." Nicole hadn't missed Janine's appraising look. She returned her smile. "Your home is exquisite." The view from the wood and stone entrance portico opened out to a gallery and living room with marble floors with an inlaid pattern.

Janine pressed her palms together, letting out her breath in a soft gasp. "Thank you, Nicole." She laid a slender hand on Zachary's arm. "But I must thank Zack for everything."

"Zack Regan and my bank account," boomed a loud male voice. "Janey, why are our guests standing there with their coats on?"

Bright color suffused Janine Prescott's fair skin as Zachary helped Nicole out of her coat, then shrugged out of his. He handed the coats to the tall, silver-haired man with the booming voice.

"If Reno's the parking attendant, then you can be coat check, Otis," Zachary said, smiling.

Otis Prescott draped their coats over the arm of his tuxedo jacket, his attention riveted on Nicole. He seemed as surprised as his wife that Zachary had come with a date, but the flicker of interest in his dark eyes was undisguised male appreciation.

Zachary saw the direction of Otis's gaze and moved closer to Nicole, his arm once again going around her waist. There was no mistaking the possessiveness in the gesture.

"Nicole, Otis Prescott, our host. Otis, Nicole Moore."

Otis's Adam's apple moved up and down his throat several times over a black bow tie before he said, "Nicole." His gaze swung back to Zachary's smug expression. "I...I'll be right back. I'll get someone to take care of your coats."

Janine cradled her swollen belly over a loosely flowing white dress. "You must forgive us, Nicole. We're usually not this impolite. I've been racing the clock." She patted her belly. "I wanted to open the house before the baby arrived."

Zachary took Janine's arm with his free hand and led her and Nicole up the marble steps to the gallery. His professional gaze took in the carefully chosen furnishings. The house was the perfect place to display the Prescotts' rare collection of Colonial American furniture.

"It should make *Architectural Digest*," he remarked, staring up at the large atrium rising through the heart of the house to the skylights in the center of the roof.

Janine affected a pout. "You ruined my surprise, Zack. They've contacted me to do a layout," she said with a wide grin.

Zachary nodded, his expression closed. "Congratulations."

"And congratulations to you, too," she crooned. "Someone from the magazine should contact you shortly. Most of the others are coming later, so why don't you show Nicole the house before they get here. I'm certain she would prefer a *private* tour from my architect."

Nicole held up the skirt to her dress as she climbed the stairs to the third floor level with Zachary. She stood beside him in the atrium, bathed in a glow of soft yellow from the recessed lighting strategically placed under clerestory windows.

"You didn't tell your friends that you were bringing a date." Her voice was soft, but not accusatory.

Zachary slipped his hands into his pockets and rocked back on his heels. His gaze met hers and held. "They didn't tell me not to." He pulled one hand from the pocket of his trousers and held it out to her. He wasn't disappointed when she took his fingers.

"This is a very special night for Otis and Janine. And it's also a very special night for me, Nikki."

Her grip tightened on the long, strong slender fingers that created structures whose style and beauty would endure and serve generations.

"You have every right to be proud of your work, Zachary, for you're truly gifted."

His fingers closed on hers, drawing her to him. "I'm not talking about my work," he replied without inflection. "I'm talking about *you*, Nicole Moore."

"Zack," she whispered, her mind spinning in a maelstrom of passion and pain.

He placed her hand over his heart. Lowering his head, his breath floated across her mouth as his heart pumped strongly under her palm. "Do you feel what you're doing to me?"

Nicole closed her eyes and swayed towards Zachary. Did he know what he was doing to her? "No," she whispered.

She wanted him. She wanted to surrender all that she had to him: the passion she knew he could elicit from her, the love she had never given to any man, and the security of her future.

Her lids fluttered, then came up as clear light brown eyes moved over Zachary's deep, mournful dark eyes, the arresting planes of his facial structure and down to the well-defined shape of his full mouth.

She knew they shared an invisible web of physical attraction, but it didn't stop there; her feelings for Zachary Regan ran deep; deep and passionate.

She tilted her chin, her mouth close to his. Her heels placed her an inch above the six-foot mark. "What am I doing to you?" she asked quietly.

Zachary released her hand and his fingers circled her waist, pulling her pliant body to his, her lace-covered breasts burning him through the starched stiffness of his shirt front. Their gazes locked as their breathing came in labored unison.

"You make me want you, Nikki," he ground out painfully between clenched teeth. "You make me want you even though I know it's wrong."

She was entranced by the torment in his eyes as she felt his vulnerability. Her hands moved from his chest to frame his lean cheeks, thumbs caressing his cheekbones.

"It's not wrong for me, Zachary," she argued softly. "What I feel for you is *not wrong*."

Zachary held his breath, praying that the physical pain would surpass his emotional pain. He hadn't wanted to—

he couldn't help it, but he had permitted Nicole to slip under his defenses. He was totally and hopelessly involved with her.

He felt his lungs burning from lack of oxygen, and let out his breath in a long, shuddering sigh.

"It's going to be all right, Zachary," she crooned. "We are going to ride the tide and let it take us wherever it leads." Nicole was caught up in her own emotions, not seeing Zachary's fear; real, naked and anguished.

He buried his face in her hair, feeding on her strength and her warmth. He wanted to believe; he had to believe her, or not only would he lose Nicole, but also himself.

His lips brushed over her hair, finding an ear. A tiny moaning sound from Nicole fired his blood. His burning mouth traced a moist path from her ear, jaw and then to the base of her throat. Zachary cradled the back of her head as she bared her neck for his tantalizing exploration.

Her lips searched and found his, parting for a healing, soul-searching kiss. He was hurting and she healed him. He hungered and she fed him. He sought love and she was there to give it to him.

Nicole pushed gently against Zachary's chest, reluctantly pulling her mouth away from his. "We must get back," she said in a husky voice, reminding him of where they were.

Zachary ran his tongue over his lips, savoring the taste of her, his gaze dropping from her face to her heaving breasts. "We'll continue our *private* tour at some other time."

Nicole nodded slowly. She had no trouble understanding his double meaning. Reaching up, she wiped away the smudge of color from his mouth with her thumb.

Zachary smiled at her, brushing her hair back into a smooth fullness around her shoulders. Reaching for her hand, he tucked it into the bend of his arm. "This house was built in 1880 as a three-story mansion, with half-timbered upper floors atop a first level of stone," he began, leading Nicole along the oval of the atrium.

Nicole listened to Zachary's mellifluous voice when they entered and left rooms as he explained how the architectural influences of Josef Hoffmann, Frank Lloyd Wright, Palladio and Baroque elements, with paired columns and the use of a square within a rectangle within an oval, came into play when he redesigned the interiors of the Prescott property. She was overwhelmed with the series of decks and terraces and a swimming pool set on a lower terrace less than two hundred feet from the water's edge of Long Island Sound.

She ran her fingers over the back of a Chippendale-style chair, smiling at Zachary. "How would you like to support Janine's obsession for antiques?"

Zachary moved behind Nicole, one hand on her shoulder, the other splayed over the flatness of her belly. She shivered when his uneven breathing caressed her neck.

"Janine doesn't have to put out more than fifteen thousand dollars for an Adams desk because she's an antique dealer."

Turning in his loose embrace, Nicole wound her arms inside his jacket and around his back. Tilting her chin, she smiled up at him through her lashes. As usual, her seductive gaze never failed to arouse him.

"Yes, Nikki. I'll ask Janine when you can see her shop," he said, reading her thoughts.

Nicole gave him a demure smile. "Thank you, Zachary."

They returned to the living room where Janine and Otis were greeting their guests with fluted glasses filled with an imported pale champagne, caviar and pate foie gras. Many other delectable canapes were served with the rich fare before the sixteen invited guests were ushered into a formal dining room for a sit-down dinner.

Zachary sat opposite Nicole, watching her charm the two men flanking her as he was relegated to explain to his dining partner how he had redesigned the gutted mansion, set on a sloping hill, into a generous, expansive house overlooking panoramic Long Island Sound.

Dinner was leisurely and relaxed, the hired caterers serving course after course of expertly prepared French dishes. Zachary caught Janine's cool gaze and nodded. This gathering would establish her reputation as a much sought-after hostess.

Dinner ended with coffee and cordials served in the enclosed solarium facing the water. The sight and sound of the icy waters crashing into the rocks and stone wall was soothing and hypnotic.

Nicole had elected to stand as she watched the frothy gray waters wash over the rocks. She detected the familiar lime fragrance of Zachary's after-shave when he stood behind her.

"Everything was very nice," she said in a quiet voice.

"Yes, it was," he agreed. "Are you ready to leave?"

Turning, she nodded. It was after midnight. "It's been a long night."

He caught her arm, smiling down at her. "Janine said she'll be happy to show you her shop next Saturday."

Nicole eyed Janine's extended belly. "If she doesn't deliver before then."

Zachary chuckled. "She still has another month before the baby's due."

Nicole doubted whether she would survive another month. "Does she have any other children beside Reno?"

"No. Reno just turned seventeen. Janine and Otis

thought Reno was going to be an only child until a doctor told Janine that what she thought was premature menopause was actually pregnancy. It came as quite a shock to Janine who's now forty-one.''

Nicole thought about herself; she was on a biological time clock. At thirty-three, she didn't have too many more years before her chances of having a baby slipped away.

Why was she thinking of bearing a child? Was it because she was getting older, or was it because of Zachary? What was it about him that made her think of love, commitment and babies?

She dismissed her musings when she and Zachary thanked their hosts and made their farewell known to the others.

Chapter Seven

Nicole melted against the leather seat as the heat filtered through the vents in the racy sports car.

"Warm enough, sweetheart?"

"Yes, thank you."

Zachary gave her a quick glance, seeing the flash of white teeth when she smiled in the dimness of the car's interior. "What should I tell Janine to put aside for you?"

"Nothing too extravagant." She mentally calculated what she could spend. "Perhaps a few serving pieces."

"Is that all?"

Nicole gave him a hostile glare. "That's all I can afford at this time, Zachary Regan."

"If you hadn't spent so much for your Adams desk you'd be able to afford more than a few serving pieces."

She crossed her arms over her chest. "Well, I didn't know you at that time, Mr. Know-It-All."

"Now that you do, I suggest that you don't buy anything else until you consult with me."

"Yes, Daddy," she replied meekly, then stuck her tongue out at him in a childish gesture.

Zachary stifled a grin. "You're pushing, Nicole," he warned in a velvety tone.

Was she pushing him? And if she was, how far could she go before he released the tight rein on his control.

Nicole knew enough about human behavior to recognize the shield Zachary had erected for himself. And he used all of the barriers: work, children and his refusal to take off his wedding band. He was sleeping with a woman, or women, but nothing beyond that. He would not permit himself to get too close or involved.

Why? She had asked herself the question over and over and had concluded that Zachary was a man who loved once, and would never love again.

Zachary took the ramp leading to the parkway, accelerating smoothly into the fast-moving traffic. "Where did your interest in antiques come from, Nikki?"

Nicole closed her eyes, smiling. "It was from my grandmother. Her house was like a museum." She reopened her eyes, still seeing the priceless treasures strewn throughout the large house. "I always went to her house after school for cookies and milk. It became a ritual that whenever I asked her about a table or serving piece, I got a history lesson.

"My great-great-great grandfather had been a skilled African sculptor who brought the knowledge of his craft with him when he made an unscheduled voyage to the Americas in the belly of a ship. He passed his skills on to his son, and in each succeeding generation there was someone who continued the tradition. I've been offered an outrageous amount of money for an ivory bracelet that has been in my family for more than two hundred and fifty years."

Zachary shifted his eyebrows. "You've never considered selling it?''

"No," she said in a firm voice. "It would be like repeating history when people were bought and sold. The pieces I've inherited are a part of my past, Zachary. They serve as a reminder of who I am and of the ties that bind my family together, generation after generation.''

Nicole told Zachary about the heirloom napkins, table-cloths, bedspreads and antique crystal, porcelain and silver packed away in her mother's attic.

He teased her, asking, "Have you thought about going into business for yourself?''

A flash of humor softened her mouth. "I have. But I don't think I'd be able to part with anything.''

"You have to know when to let go," Zachary said.

She stared at him, her delicate jaw clenched. "You're a fine one to talk, Zachary. When are you going to let go of your past?''

Nicole watched Zachary warily, expecting him to lash out at her. He surprised her, replying, "I'm trying, Nikki.''

She covered his right hand on the steering wheel, squeezing his fingers gently. "If you have a problem you want to talk out, I'm here for you.''

Zachary managed a sad smile. What Nicole didn't know was she was the 'problem'. Her nearness sent his senses spinning out of control, her wit made him laugh, and her femininity made him aware of his maleness as no other woman had ever done before.

He pulled his hand from under hers, capturing her fingers. He brought her hand to his mouth and placed a kiss on each finger. "What am I going to do with you, Nicole Moore?''

Exhaling softly, Nicole smiled dreamily. *Love me,* she thought, but said instead, "I don't know.''

An easy, light mood enveloped them on the return drive to Manhattan. Nicole and Zachary sang along with a radio station, pantomiming the antics of the artists they were familiar with. Zachary remembered the words to most of the old Motown favorites that had been popular when he attended the fraternity parties at Howard. Their musical session ended with a stirring rendition of *"Baby I Need Your Loving,"* a popular Four Tops hit.

Zachary parked the car in front of the high-rise complex, shaking his head and laughing. "We make a pretty good team, Nikki."

Nicole spread her hands out, palms upward, and smiled. "Thank you, ladies and gentlemen. We appreciate your kindness tonight. Zachary and I thank you, The Pips thank you, The Supremes thank you and The Vandellas thank you."

Drawn into her playful mood, Zachary added, "The Miracles and The Temptations also thank you for your generous applause."

They looked at one another, dissolving into a spasm of laughter. It had been a long time, too long, since Zachary had felt that free and alive. When he first saw Nicole in the restaurant two weeks before, he never would've suspected she could be so uninhibited. Uninhibited, yet controlled.

Zachary thought he was an expert when it came to controlling his emotions, but Nicole had proven him wrong. Her hot mouth wrung spasms of passion from him, then like quicksilver she withdrew her sensual spell, leaving him wanting more and more of her until he thought he would dissolve in a swirling current of frustration.

"We missed our calling," Nicole said to Zachary as they walked to the entrance of her building. "We could've given Marvin Gaye and Tammy Terrell some stiff competition."

Zachary pulled her closer to his side. "It's not too late."

She smiled up at him. "It's too late for me. I could never begin to imitate the moves of these hip-hop dancers and rappers."

"All we'd need is a pair of harem pants, Nikki. M.C. Hammer would have nothing on us."

Nicole gave him a surprised look. "What would a conservative old architect like you know about M.C. Hammer?" she teased.

He managed to look insulted. "I'm not that old or that conservative. You must remember I have a pre-teen daughter who thinks MTV is the only channel on the dial."

Nicole nodded at the doorman on duty. "You must have an interesting household," she remarked once she and Zachary were in the elevator.

"Strange would be more appropriate," Zachary said firmly.

"I don't believe you."

Zachary leaned against the elevator wall, one ankle crossed over the other. "Even the dog is weird. Max and David talk to one another."

Nicole was hard pressed not to laugh. "You're weird if you believe that."

Zachary moved closer to her, his breath stirring the hair on her forehead. "All of the Regans are strange."

"You're not strange," she countered. "You're..."

"I'm what, Nikki?" His voice had lowered with his lids. The elevator doors opened and Zachary caught her arm in a protective hold. "I'm what?" he repeated as they made their way slowly down the hall.

Nicole handed him her key and watched him unlock the door. "You're very nice," she finally said when he pushed against the door.

Zachary pulled her inside the apartment, locking the door behind them. His towering height and broad shoulders made the space in the entry appear smaller than it was when Nicole opened the closet. She removed a hanger and Zachary helped her out of her coat. He hung both of their coats in the closet and followed her into the living room.

Nicole kicked off her shoes and sank down to the firm softness of the love seat. Zachary sat beside her, his hands sweeping under her calves and cradling her stockinged feet in his lap.

Closing her eyes, she rested her head against the plump cushion. "That feels good," she sighed when he massaged her toes, arch and ankle of one foot, then the other. The warmth from his strong fingers shot up her legs and she inhaled sharply. "You cook and give a wonderful massage," she crooned. "What other talents are you hiding?"

"Not much else," he replied, staring at her composed features.

"I don't believe you."

His hands moved up to her knees. "Believe me."

Nicole's eyes reopened quickly. His fingers were splayed over her thigh and her skin tingled from the intimate contact.

"Please undo the middle buttons on my dress. I'll be able to manage the rest." She extracted her legs from his loose grip and swung them to the floor, shifting and presenting Zachary with her back.

Her breath stopped, suspended on a slender thread of erotic longing. Zachary had swept her hair aside and brushed his lips over the back of her neck.

"One," he whispered as he undid the top button, then kissed her bare flesh. "Two," he continued, repeating the feathery gesture, his lips grazing her sensitive skin.

The heat of his mouth alternated with the coolness of her exposed body as his tongue trailed a moist path down her spine. Nicole tried wiggling off the love seat, struggling futilely against his superior strength when he curved an arm around her waist.

He undid the last button, and her back lay bare to his rapacious mouth. He rose smoothly, both hands spanning her waist, and pulled her to her feet. He pressed his chest against her back, the studs on his shirt biting into her tender skin.

"Go change, Nikki," he ordered hoarsely.

Nicole needed no further urging. He released her and she picked up her shoes and headed for the bedroom. Closing the door, she sagged weakly against it.

He's teasing me! He's playing with me again, she thought wildly. Nicole didn't know who she was more afraid of: herself or Zachary. Being with him was thrilling and frightening, frightening because what she was experiencing with Zachary Regan was foreign and wildly primitive.

Lust! The word froze in her brain. For the first time in her adult life the basic urge to mate shook her to the core.

Then her analytical training surfaced, reminding her that she wanted Zachary because she couldn't have him.

A sad smile pulled her mouth down at the corners. Her mother had predicted it. Margaret Moore had complained that she was too picky whenever Nicole rejected a man Margaret considered suitable as a potential husband for her daughter. Exasperated, Margaret would pout for days, then say sagely, "What may be good to you may not be good for you."

How right you are, Nicole mused, pushing off the door.

Zachary made her feel good, but in the long run he would offer her nothing. As much as she wanted Zachary she was unwilling to give him more than she could hope to receive in return. Their relationship could not be that unbalanced.

She slipped out of her dress and panty hose, changing into a red sweatsuit. Numerous washings had faded the college logo across her breasts. She removed her earrings and secured her hair in an elastic band on the top of her head. By the time she left the bedroom, she had regained her composure.

"It smells good," she remarked, walking into the kitchen.

Zachary having removed his glasses, jacket and tie, sat on the tall stool watching the automatic coffee maker brewing the rich imported Brazilian coffee she had received as a Christmas grab bag gift at the center. His lounging stance, one patent slippered foot anchored on the floor, the other on the stool rung, epitomized raw masculine grace. He was equally virile in formal or casual attire.

"I hope you don't mind that I opened the package."

Smiling, Nicole shook her head. "Not at all. I was looking forward to testing it."

He arched an eyebrow. "You have a coffee maker. Why don't you use it?"

"I usually make instant. It's hard to botch a cup of instant coffee." She reached into an overhead cabinet for cups.

Zachary's gaze moved slowly over her slim, sweatsuit-clad body. Within minutes Nicole had transformed from a sleek, composed, sophisticated woman to an ethereal ingenue with bare feet and her hair swept up in an elastic band on the top of her head. He didn't know which image he preferred, for he knew under both Nicoles was a simmering passion straining to surface if only she willed it.

He had felt her restrained passion and her soothing empathy. He longed to open up to her, telling her of his apprehension and phobia. More than anything else, Zachary yearned to tell Nicole that he wanted her; wanted her in a way a man wanted a woman; and he wanted to tell her that he needed her; needed her more than he'd ever needed any woman, including Julie.

He wanted to entrust his life and his future to her. The notion shocked him as he sprang to his feet, startling Nicole. She dropped a saucer, the delicate plate shattering into minute pieces around her bare feet.

Zachary moved quickly, an arm going around her waist and lifting her high off the floor. "I'm sorry," he apologized in a deep, hoarse tone.

Nicole's arms circled Zachary's neck, her head level with his. She tightened her grip, not wanting to be separated from him and luxuriating in his warmth and strength as he held her effortlessly with one arm.

Her heart fluttered wildly in her chest as she felt his thudding strongly against her own. A tingle of excitement shattered the shield she had erected against Zachary Regan, and a tremor of desire pulsed uncontrollably throughout her body. A torrent of passion skidded and whirled, making her weak with the delicious heat warming and flooding the source of her womanhood.

"Put me down, Zachary," she ordered in a silky voice.

Zachary struggled valiantly to bring his own runaway emotions under control. The softness of Nicole's body, the fragrance of her perfume and the large burnt-sienna brown eyes peering deeply into his own drugged him. His left arm circled her waist, making her his prisoner.

"Where?"

She blinked once. "Where what?"

Zachary's breathing came in a shuddering rush. "Where do you want me to put you down?"

Nicole closed her eyes. She knew what he wanted; she knew that he wanted to make love to her. It couldn't happen, because if she made love to Zachary there would be no turning back, no walking away from him. It had only taken seconds for her to realize that she was falling in love with a man who didn't love her and who didn't *want* to love her.

He didn't even need her. They were attracted to one another, had enjoyed each other's company, therefore it was normal that physical desire had been strong between them; a desire Zachary could feel with *any* woman. But she didn't intend to be *any woman*. The sooner Zachary learned that, the better it would be for him.

Her eyes reopened and she pressed a kiss at the corner of his sensual mouth. "My bedroom," she replied in a throaty drawl. Zachary shifted, cradling one arm under her knees. Nicole smiled, pressing her cheek against his shoulder. "I want to get a pair of shoes, then I'll clean up the glass."

He almost dropped her. In the instant that Nicole had mentioned her bedroom, Zachary had forgotten his pledge not to become involved with her. He wanted to make love to her, and he was ready to let her into his life. He had gambled and lost. And this was one time he was grateful for the loss.

He walked into her bedroom and set her on her feet. Without saying a word, he turned and walked away, leaving Nicole staring at his back. She knew by the set of his jaw and his stiff back that he was upset.

Nicole made her way to a walk-in closet and slipped her bare feet into a pair of worn canvas deck shoes. What did he expect from her? He had told her what he felt for her was wrong. There was no way she was going to offer her love to a man who was in love with another woman; a woman who reached beyond the grave to hold him captive.

She returned to the kitchen, but discovered that Zachary had found a broom and dustpan in the narrow closet and had swept up the shattered saucer. He appeared to be as much at home in the kitchen as he was in his office leaning over a drawing board.

He emptied the dustpan in a shiny black lacquered wastebasket. "I think I got all of it up, but I suggest you wear shoes in here for a few days to make certain."

Nicole met his solemn expression with one of her own. Their easygoing camaraderie was gone. Desire and denial had reared its head, turning them into cautious strangers.

She reached up into the cabinet for another saucer, but Zachary caught her hand. "How valuable was it, Nicole?"

"Not very valuable," she countered, staring at his strong fingers circling her waist.

He released her, reaching into the cabinet. He withdrew a matching saucer and turned it over. His eyes widened behind his lenses when he read the printing stamped on the underside. "Limoges is not something you'd pick up on a sale table at a department store, Nicole."

"No big deal, Zachary," she said, taking the saucer from his loose grip.

Zachary recaptured her hand and took the saucer. He placed it on the counter behind her. Both hands went to her shoulders, pulling her up close to his chest. "Is anything a big deal, Nicole? The only thing that seems to spark any excitement in you is your job. It's as if you've erected a wall around you, and you dare anyone to try to scale it."

Nicole managed a smile, infuriating Zachary. Then her gaze narrowed as she raised her dimpled chin. "Are you talking about yourself, Zachary?" She didn't wait for his answer, saying, "You're a fine one to talk, Zachary Regan. You give me the line that you don't wnat to get involved, but you are. You want me, yet you feel that it's wrong to want me. The feeling is mutual, because I don't want anyone who doesn't want me. I am not that needy or desperate for a man."

He loosened his hold, his hands moving down her back to her waist. Lowering his head, he buried his face in her hair. She shivered when his hot breath fanned her neck.

"I do want you, Nikki," he groaned painfully.

Nicole's arms circled his slim waist. "Then why don't you let me in, Zachary?" She heard his quick intake of breath. Pulling back, she glanced up, studying his face intently and watching the play of emotions on his features. The twitching muscle in his jaw eased, the hard line of his full mouth softened and the heat of his gaze devoured her whole.

"Whether you know it or not, you're in," he stated quietly. "You're in, Nikki," he repeated, covering her mouth with his, sealing his confession.

Nicole melted in his embrace and surrendered to the intimacy of the moment. She kissed him with a hunger she hadn't known she was capable of. Her tongue searched his tongue, teeth, then his firm masterful lips.

Zachary returned her greedy kiss, drawing from her what he had always sought in a woman: unbridled passion. His hands slipped down, cradling the slim roundness of her hips in his splayed fingers and bringing her against the swelling hardness between his thighs.

"I want you," he groaned against her mouth. "Yet I can't put into words what kind of wanting it is. I want to see you," he continued, grinding his pelvis against hers. "Every day. I want to hear your soft Southern drawl that slips through when I least expect it. And I know that I can't keep my hands off of you." Easing her back, he studied her shocked expression. "I want to kiss you, Nikki. All over." Zachary smiled when a soft gasp escaped her. "There's not one part of your body I don't want to touch or taste."

The muscles in Nicole's stomach clenched tightly and she swallowed back her apprehension at his erotic admission. She wanted to believe him, but what frightened her was that she didn't want to live in a dead woman's shadow.

Thick black lashes came down and hid her gaze from his, successfully shutting him out and Zachary felt his own fear spiral.

Zachary watched the sweep of her lashes touch her high, sculpted cheekbones. The lines and curves of her face were perfect. Her forehead was high and slightly rounded, providing a symmetrical background for sweeping naturally arching eyebrows over large expressive gold-brown eyes. Her lashes were long and full, eliminating the need for a thick coating of mascara.

He traced the curve of a cheekbone from her ear to a nose that was short and straight enough to be labeled as cute. But it was her mouth and chin that held him enthralled. Her mouth was wide, full, lush and sexy; sexy and hypnotic. His finger grazed the slight indentation in her chin.

"Do you want me, Nicole?"

Nicole tried to bring her confused emotions into some semblance of order. Since she had met Zachary she found herself unbalanced. Just when she thought she could lower her defenses and relax, he changed direction. Everything that was safe and protective told her not to continue to see him, and she wondered when she had become so reckless as to embark on a journey of self-destruction.

Ignoring the little warning voice in her head, she replied, "Yes, I do want you."

He released her and stared down into her luminous eyes. The look of a supremely satisfied and confident male softened his features. Crossing his arms over the front of his starched tuxedo shirt, he smiled. "Good. At least we can both agree on what we want."

Turning away from him, Nicole wrapped her arms around her body in a protective gesture. She jumped when Zachary's hands touched her shoulders. His hot breath seared her neck through a curtain of thick hair.

"It's all right, Nikki. Everything is going to be all right."

She spun around, her steady gaze moving over his face. "Will it?" There was no mistaking her frustration.

Slipping both hands into the pockets of his dress trousers, Zachary shrugged his shoulders in a nonchalant gesture. A slight smile touched his mobile mouth. "Yes, it will," he answered with a maddening arrogance. "I'll make certain of that."

Nicole called on the vestiges of whatever pride she had left. "Have you decided to set up the conditions of this so-called relationship, or do you intend to solicit my input?"

"It takes two to have a relationship, Nicole." An icy chill lingered after his statement.

She laughed. The sound was false and filled with contempt. "It's nice that you can remember that."

"What is it you want?" he asked, his sharp tone mirroring his own anger.

Nicole felt in control for the first time since her brother introduced her to Zachary Regan. Her smile was seductive, but her eyes were brimming with rage. "Take off your wedding ring."

They stared at one another, the seconds stretching into a minute and beyond. An expressive glow of satisfaction changed Nicole, inward and outwardly. She felt Zachary's inner battle as surely as if it was her own. He had not removed his hands from his pockets.

"All right, Zachary. You don't have to," she stated in a firm voice. "But don't you ever expect me to do what I don't want to do. And that includes everything," she added, punctuating each word with a jab of her forefinger to the center of his hard chest. "Now will you please go home. I've enjoyed our evening together, but I need my sleep." A delicate yawn confirmed her order.

Zachary didn't know whether to laugh or rip the clothes from her body and make love to her on the kitchen floor. She was the most exasperating woman he'd ever met. Strong-willed, spoiled, opinionated and challenging. She hadn't asked him to remove his ring, but demanded he do so.

But what Nicole didn't know was that Zachary was her equal. He gave her a slow, sinister smile. "I'm leaving, Nikki. You've just used your second strike, because this will be the last time you'll order me to leave your place."

He didn't give Nicole a chance to reply when he turned and walked out of the kitchen. She followed him to the door and watched him pull on his duster. The long black silk coat swept elegantly around his legs when he turned to face her.

"It's been an interesting evening, Nikki."

Nicole took a step forward and tilted her chin. "That it has," she agreed softly.

She didn't protest when he reached out and caught her hand in his. Bringing her fingers to his mouth, he pressed a moist kiss to her palm.

Nicole sighed heavily at the feathery sensations coursing up and down her arm. Her free hand caught the one holding hers tightly.

"Good night, Zachary," she breathed out, her voice dropping to a lower register.

Zachary released her, but not before he felt her trembling. "Good night, Nikki, and thanks for your company." He unlocked and opened the door.

"Drive safely," Nicole urged when he winked and smiled down at her.

"I'll call you tomorrow," he promised.

Nicole nodded, then closed the door behind him. Zachary was right; the night had been interesting. Quite interesting indeed.

Both of them had admitted that they wanted each other, and Nicole had established that she was in control of where she wanted the relationship to go; she had to establish that or she would do all of the giving.

She had given once, not receiving in return. It would not happen again.

Chapter Eight

Nicole sat on the wooden bench, squinting at Vera through a haze of steam. She inhaled deeply, filling her lungs with moist heat. The sauna was working. The tightness in her arms and legs were easing.

She had neglected her weekly workout sessions. She tried to visit the health club at least three times a week, but lately she was lucky if she made it one day out of seven.

"This is the best gift I've ever received," Vera said, lying on the bench, eyes closed. "That's what I love about you, Nick. Practicality. Everyone else gives me bathrobes, slippers and blouses for Christmas, but not you. You knew exactly what I needed. A health club membership."

Nicole swung her legs over the bench and eased her body into a prone position. "That's me. Miss Practicality."

Vera turned her head and looked at Nicole. "How practical are you with Zachary Regan?"

A slight smile curved her full mouth. "Not practical at all." She pulled the towel up higher over her breasts. "I think I'm falling for him."

Vera sat up quickly, holding her own towel in place. The steam had plastered her curling hair to her scalp.

"You're what?"

"You heard me, Vera. The man has gotten to me."

"Oh no," Vera moaned.

"Oh yes," Nicole retorted.

"Is it good?" Vera's eyes were flashing with excitement.

"The question should be, is he good?"

Vera's mouth formed a perfect O. "Are you sleeping with him?"

It was Nicole's turn to sit up. "Of course not."

"And why not?"

"Because it's not *that* good," she retorted.

Vera folded her hands on her hips. "Girl, talk to me. You're not making sense."

"Zachary *is* good. In fact, very good. He's brilliant, gorgeous, sexy and..."

"In that order?" Vera asked, interrupting.

Nicole pursed her lips, appearing to be deep in thought. She shook her head. "No."

"Then he's sexy first?"

"V-e-r-y sexy," Nicole confirmed with a wide grin.

"Are you going to let him get away?"

Now Nicole was confused. "I don't follow you, Vera."

Vera moved over to Nicole's bench, not wanting the other women in the room to overhear their conversation. "I've been thinking about this for a long time, and now it's time I got it off my chest. I think you're too repressed, Nick. Let me finish," she said when Nicole opened her mouth to refute her assessment of her.

"We shared an apartment for more than four years, and in all of that time I don't remember you ever talking about a man being sexy. Even when you thought you were in love with Gene, there was no sparkle or excitement between the two of you."

Vera was right. There was no excitement between her and Gene because he demanded so much attention that there were times when she refused to see him.

"Zachary is *not* Gene," Nicole stated firmly.

"That I have no doubt. And despite all you've told me about his not wanting to get involved you've gone and fallen for the man."

"We've passed the 'not getting involved' stage. We're seeing one another," Nicole informed Vera.

"On a regular basis?"

It was almost a week since she had attended the Prescott dinner party with Zachary, and in that time she and Zachary had met twice for breakfast and once for dinner.

"Somewhat regular."

"And?"

"And what, Vera?"

Vera glanced around and moved closer to Nicole. "He hasn't tried to..."

"Seduce me?" Vera nodded. "You're a worse busybody than my mother," Nicole chided.

"Come on, Nick," Vera pleaded.

"That's too personal, Vera."

"You can trust me, Nick. You're like my sister."

Nicole gave her a pained look. "There are things even sisters don't tell one another."

Vera folded her arms over her chest, pouting. She looked more twenty-one than thirty-one.

Nicole hugged her, laughing. "The day I jump his bones, you'll probably be the first to know."

"You promise, Nick?"

"I'll think about it."

Vera returned to her bench and they lay in the heat-filled room for another fifteen minutes before heading for the showers.

Nicole towel dried her hair and pushed it up under a knitted cap, while Vera dried her short-cut hair quickly with a small hand dryer.

Both were dressed in running shoes, jeans and heavy sweaters under their coats when they left the health club and walked back to Vera's apartment. The weather had warmed, the mercury rising out of the teens for the first time in weeks.

Nicole felt invigorated. Swimming and jogging for more than two hours was what she needed to unwind at the end of a demanding work week. She had covered for a social worker who had fallen and broken her ankle. It would be another two weeks before the woman would be able to return to work, but with the aid of a cane.

Vera groaned the minute she stepped into her building's vestibule. There was a large printed sign posted over the mailboxes. There would be no heat or hot water because of a broken pipe.

"I can't survive without hot water, Nick," Vera wailed.

"You can stay with me this weekend," Nicole offered.

Vera gave her a forlorn look. "You don't mind?"

"Of course not. What are sisters for?"

"And you're the best, even if you're sex-starved."

"Speak for yourself, Vera Walker," Nicole teased, following Vera up the four flights. "Since you've stopped seeing Adam I don't think you've been too *busy* with any one man."

"You're right about that," Vera confirmed over her shoulder.

Nicole stepped into her old apartment, experiencing a wealth of old memories. It was small, clean and homey. But right now it was cold with the absence of heat coming through the radiators.

Nicole collected her handbag and waited for Vera to pack a small bag with clothes for the weekend. Vera packed in record time and less than forty minutes later she and Nicole peeled off their heavy clothing after settling into the warm apartment high above the streets of Manhattan's East Harlem.

They reverted back to their old habit of drinking coffee, listening to music and talking for hours. Nicole slid off the love seat, standing and stretching out her cramped limbs.

"You can take the bed tonight. I'll sleep out here on the love seat."

Vera fluffed up her short hair, shaking her head. "No way. I don't mind sleeping out here."

"I have to be up early and I don't want to wake you up." Nicole grimaced when she noted the time. It was nearly one, and Zachary was scheduled to pick her up at eight.

"Where are you going?" Vera asked between yawns.

Nicole removed the cushions from the love seat and stacked them on the floor. "Zachary's taking me to an antique shop out on Long Island."

Vera gave her a Cheshire cat grin. "Don't tell me I'll get to meet the very sexy Zachary Regan in the flesh."

Nicole couldn't stop a smile from crinkling her eyes. "Go to bed, Vera."

Vera yawned again. "I'm going, but you'd better not attempt to sneak out of here before I get a chance to lay these peepers on your boyfriend."

Leaning down, Nicole pulled out the convertible bed. "Zachary's not my boyfriend."

"Carson Bates is *not* your boyfriend."

"Carson is my friend."

"How right you are, Nick. Friends are comfortable and

non-threatening. And from what you've said about Zachary, the man appears to be threatening to your emotional stability. Good night," she said quickly, not giving Nicole the chance to come back with a retort.

Nicole watched Vera retreat to the bedroom while she made her way to a closet to retrieve bedding for her bed. Vera was right. Zachary was dangerous. The forbidden fruit had become more tempting each time she saw him.

It seemed as if her head had just touched the pillow when Nicole awoke to streams of daylight pouring through the partially-drawn drapes. She groaned when she looked at the clock on her desk. She had to get up and be ready for Zachary. Janine Prescott was opening her shop early to give them a private showing.

Nicole showered, blew out her hair, curled her bangs with a curling iron, secured the back in a French braid and managed to dress all within half an hour.

The intercom buzzed exactly at eight o'clock. Nicole answered the ring and waited. Minutes later Zachary's tall form stepped into the entry.

"Good morning," he murmured, pressing his lips to her forehead.

Nicole touched her lips to his smooth, freshly-shaved jaw. "Good morning. I have company," she informed him in a low, soft voice.

A fleeting shadow of rage swept through Zachary, but he successfully concealed it from Nicole. He didn't want to believe that she had slept with another man while appearing so unaffected by it.

But she had warned him. She would see him when she wasn't occupied with other things and other people. It was something he had to accept, or not see her; and not once had he thought about not seeing her.

Their relationship had undergone a change since the Prescott dinner party. It had become smoother, more comfortable, when they lapsed into an almost platonic existence.

"If you had other plans, you should've called me," Zachary said tersely.

"I don't have any plans," Nicole replied.

"You have *company.*"

Nicole wanted to scream at him when she heard his censuring tone. Her eyes narrowed to angry slits. "You think I have a man here, don't you?"

Zachary slipped his hands into the pockets of his slacks and rocked back on his heels. His frown and silence confirmed her query.

"You..."

"What the hell am I supposed to think, Nicole?" he rasped angrily, cutting her off. "You're seeing another man, and I assumed you're..." He let his words trail off.

Nicole hadn't gone out with Carson since the day of the Super Bowl, but she wasn't about to tell Zachary that. "And you assumed that that man spent the night with me," she finished for him.

"You're so foolish, Zachary Regan," she said quietly. *I'm in love with you,* she thought. How could she sleep with another man when she loved him?

Vera walked into the living room, wearing a white sweatshirt and matching pants. Zachary's shock was apparent when he stared at the petite feminine figure.

Vera drew in a soft breath, returning Zachary's stare. He was casually dressed in a short suede jacket, wool slacks and a pullover sweater in brown and green shades, bringing attention to the lean, hard lines of his masculine physique. Zachary flashed a slow smile, displaying the single dimple in his cheek and Vera gasped audibly.

He nodded. "Good morning," he said smoothly.

"Hi," Vera squeaked. She cleared her throat, looking embarrassed. She had been caught staring, with her mouth open. "Good morning. I'm Vera Walker, Nick's ex-roommate."

Zachary took several steps and extended his hand. "Zachary Regan."

Vera took the proffered hand. "It's nice meeting you. I've heard so much about you."

Zachary arched an eyebrow at Nicole. "You don't say?"

"I do say." Vera had recovered from her initial shock of seeing Zachary Regan. Nicole had lied to her. He was more than gorgeous. He was arrogantly male.

Vera ignored Nicole's frown, saying, "Nick told me that you'll be hiring two of my students for her work-study program."

Zachary released Vera's hand and smiled again. "The decision is not going to be an easy one to make. All of the candidates are superior students."

"If that's the case, why don't you hire all of them?" Nicole replied.

"That sounds like a good idea," Vera said quickly.

Zachary's glance darted from Vera to Nicole. "Am I missing something? I agreed to take on two students. How did I get to four?"

"Two plus two equals four," Nicole crooned in a soft tone.

Zachary's expression was closed. "I know how to count, Nicole."

Nicole moved over and patted his smooth cheek. "Don't be such a grouch this morning, darling. We were only joking."

Zachary caught Nicole's fingers in a firm grip. He stared down into her eyes. He was still flustered because he thought she had spent the night with a man. And it was the first time he'd ever experienced jealousy. Raw, ugly jealousy.

"I'm a bear because I haven't had my first cup of coffee," he said between clenched teeth.

"If you want to wait I can put up a pot," Vera volunteered.

Nicole held onto Zachary's wrist, forcing him to release hers. "That's all right, Vera. We'll get some from the corner deli." She walked to the closet in the entry and pulled out a navy pea jacket. Slipping her arms into the sleeves, she smiled at Zachary. "Come, Papa Bear. Let's get some coffee into you before you start growling again."

Zachary winked at Vera. "I'm only dangerous when I stop growling."

"Have fun," Vera called out when Nicole opened the door.

"Nice meeting you, Vera," Zachary said over his shoulder.

"Same here," Vera replied, smiling.

Nicole and Zachary walked down the hall to the elevators. She waited until the doors closed behind them before saying, "What's bothering you, Zachary?"

He leaned against the opposite wall of the elevator, noticing the slight frown marring her smooth forehead. "I need coffee," he insisted, not wanting to reveal that she was bothering him.

Her frown deepened. "Remind me never to wake you up."

"Why not?"

Shrugging her shoulders, Nicole turned away from him. "Because you really know how to tie on a blue funk."

"A blue what?"

"An attitude; a bad mood, Zachary," she explained.

He studied her delicate profile, grinning broadly. "Maybe if you *did* wake me up I'd be in a better mood."

Nicole watched the overhead dial light up the column of numbers as the elevator made its descent to the lobby. "No thanks."

Zachary moved behind her, his warm breath caressing her ear. "What are you afraid of, Nikki? That once you try me you wouldn't want to give me up?"

She glanced up at him over her shoulder. "I see you still haven't let the air out of your head."

He touched his lips to her hair. "I don't see why I should, *darling*. I've never had any complaints, Nikki," he whispered softly.

Nicole was laughing when the elevator doors opened. "I must say you're original. Usually it's baby, oh baby, if you don't give me some I'll just die. Or either it's I've got something special. Real special, mama. You've just got to try it."

Zachary laughed with her, pulling her hand into the bend of his arm as they made their way across the lobby and out of the building.

"I suppose you've heard them all."

She nodded. "From the time I was old enough to understand the strange mating habits of human beings."

He smiled down at her when she tilted her chin. "And you survived."

She couldn't meet his gaze. His mouth was smiling, but his eyes weren't. They were brimming with a curious intensity that beckoned her to throw caution to the wind and accept his veiled invitation.

"Yes, Zachary. I've survived." Her voice was even and void of expression.

"How much longer will you continue to survive?"

"Only I will know that."

"Perhaps, Nikki. Perhaps." He tightened his hold on her hand. "I suppose I'll have to do with coffee *this morning.*"

"Make it strong and black, Zachary," she warned with a sensual smile. "You're going to need it."

Nicole and Zachary ordered containers of coffee from a small delicatessen already filled with regular customers who stopped in for the breakfast specials. At the last moment they decided to share a large bran muffin.

Minutes later Nicole sat beside Zachary, feeding him small pieces of the muffin while he steered his car through the increasing city traffic.

"Don't get too used to this preferential treatment," she teased after he'd licked the remaining crumbs from her fingers.

He gave her a quick glance. "I'll return the favor one day. That's a promise," he added when she flashed him a skeptical look.

"No promises. We don't want to become too involved." He cursed softly under his breath and she laughed. "Would you please elaborate on that expletive, Zachary?"

"You wouldn't want to know."

Nicole stared at his solemn expression. Zachary had lied to her; something was bothering him.

"I do want to know."

He managed a brittle smile. "You're not making it easy for me, Dr. Moore. I need a couch to recline on when

I bare my soul to you.''

"That can be arranged.''

Zachary stopped for a red light and draped his right arm over the back of Nicole's seat. His grin was sinister. "When?"

"You set the time and I'll oblige you,'' she offered.

"It'll be soon.'' It had to be soon or else he was going to have a breakdown.

Zachary took the container of coffee from Nicole, sipping the strong black liquid through the small slot torn in the plastic top. It was hot and soothing, sliding down the back of his throat and warming his chest. A feeling of well-being flowed through him and he felt his tension easing. It wasn't just the coffee, but Nicole. Having her next to him and knowing he would spend most of the day with her had filled him with an almost childlike euphoric exuberance.

He was relaxed; more relaxed than he had been in a long time. Nicole Moore had unknowingly become a calming balm, a stabilizer.

You need someone other than your children. Someone with some permanence; a woman who wouldn't be available just for your physical needs. A woman you can laugh with. A woman you can love, and who'll love you in return.

Her words were branded in his brain. Was she that woman? Was she the woman he could love and have her love him in return?''

Was she talking about herself or some other nameless, faceless woman in his future. But then Zachary realized that he didn't want another woman; he wanted Nicole; only Nicole.

Was the feeling reciprocated? Did she want him?

Of course not, he thought. How could she when she continued to see other men. Again the alien emotion of jealousy pierced his being.

"Do you have anything planned for Valentine's Day?" he asked without warning.

Nicole turned her head slowly, staring at his tense jaw. Her gaze lingered on the strongly sculptured bones, making for an arresting face.

"Yes," she answered quietly. "I'd planned to take in dinner and a live show at Fat Tuesday's. Why do you ask?"

Zachary shrugged a broad shoulder under his pullover sweater. "I just thought maybe you'd want to do something special, that's all."

"Don't you think of dining at Fat Tuesday's as something special? I think it's quite appropriate with the Lenten season the next week."

Zachary flipped a token into the wire basket at the bridge's toll booth. Cold air quickly filled the car's interior until he pressed a button, raising the window. "It's okay," he mumbled under his breath.

She forced back a smile. "What do you consider special?"

"I was thinking about the '21' Club or the Rainbow Room."

Nicole shook her head. "Not intimate enough. I prefer to celebrate in a less formal, more relaxing atmosphere and I thought you would too."

Zachary took his gaze off the road for a second. Nicole flashed him a sensual smile. "Are you asking me out, Nikki?"

"I was going to," she replied softly.

"Well." The dimple winked in his right cheek when he smiled.

"Well what, Zachary?"

"Ask me, Nikki."

"No."

His smile vanished. "Why not?" He shot her an angry scowl.

"Because I wasn't ready to ask you," she teased. "You jumped the gun."

Zachary counted slowly to himself. Nicole wasn't going to make it easy for him. But then she hadn't been easy about anything that concerned their personal relationship. He'd hoped things would go as smoothly as they had with their business dealings.

"I wanted to ask you before your other *men* did," he stated with heavy sarcasm.

"Don't worry about my other men, Zachary," she retorted, not registering the jealous undertones in his words. "Valentine's Day is yours, darling."

"Thanks," Zachary grunted.

It was the second time that morning that she had called him darling. And Zachary wondered if she called all of her men darling.

He hated her other men. Men who talked to her, admired her and some who may have possibly touched her.

She's mine. Mine and mine alone.

He hadn't thought he could be that possessive, but then he was discovering quirks about Zachary Regan he hadn't known existed. Knowing Nicole had led him to do a lot of soul-searching and self-examining; and what he had come up with was startling. His feelings for her ran deep; deep, raw and passionate.

Zachary sat on a ladderback armchair, watching Nicole. She smiled at Janine Prescott, nodding her head. She had decided to buy a gold enameled turquoise snuff box. *So much for serving pieces,* he thought.

He found her enchanting. Today she wore a pair of low-heeled black riding boots, a calf-length navy pleated skirt stitched down at the hip, a white linen blouse with a lacy cutwork collar and a navy V-neck cardigan. She had foregone makeup, except for a subtle hint of red color for her lips.

Nicole walked over to Zachary when Janine went to the back of the elegant antique shop to direct her stockperson to wrap up the snuff box.

Zachary extended his hands, capturing her fingers and pulling her to his side when he rose to his feet. Smiling down at her radiant face, he said, "Wonderful choice."

Nicole pressed her forehead to his shoulder. "It's perfect."

You're perfect, Zachary thought. Nicole was the perfect woman, and she would make the perfect wife.

He stiffened and Nicole was aware of the changes in him immediately. Pulling back, she watched his expressive face change and become almost somber. The fingers of her right hand moved up and grazed his jaw. He jerked as if her fingers were hot tongs.

"What's the matter, Zachary?" she asked quietly.

Releasing her hand, he turned his back. "Nothing."

Nicole stepped around him, peering closely and seeing his anguished gaze. "Are you certain?"

He forced a smile. "Yes," he lied. He wasn't okay. Pain and fear attacked him, and it was all he could do not to blurt out that he had fallen in love with her. And what he feared most had surfaced again. Every woman he loved he lost.

Zachary registered genuine concern in Nicole's eyes, experiencing guilt. Why had he continued to keep her off-balance? Why hadn't he been able to tell her of his phobia? She would understand; she had to understand. Why couldn't he trust her enough to unburden himself?

He had to try. He had to begin now.

A slow smile softened his face. "How would you like to meet my children?"

A different kind of uneasiness was transferred to Nicole. When Zachary had mentioned he would show her where he lived she took that to mean his neighborhood, not his children.

Her feelings for him were becoming more confused. For all of his protests about not becoming involved with one another, they were.

"Do you want me to?" she asked, answering his question with one of her own.

"Yes," Zachary answered smoothly.

Nicole wondered how much more would she be forced to share with Zachary Regan before she decided to end their relationship. It was reaching the stage when she knew further involvement would be an open invitation to real pain.

I'll know when to stop it, she reassured herself. *I'll know when I'm in too deep.* She would remain in control—at all times.

Believing this, she said, "I'd love to meet them."

Chapter Nine

Zachary's hand hit the horn twice and he maneuvered into the driveway to a carriage house converted for family living. There came a loud barking, followed by the appearance of a large German shepherd. He raced back and forth along a lower deck, a flash of gold and black fur.

Zachary shut off the car's engine and smiled at Nicole. "Max's bark is worse than his bite. You're safe as long as you don't touch him. You have to let him come to you."

Then Max wasn't much different from his master, Nicole thought. She was safe from Zachary as long as he didn't touch her. A kiss or the crush of his body and she was lost in the passion he evoked so effortlessly.

She waited for Zachary to help her from the car, walking close to him when he led the way up a flight of stairs to the second level.

A glass door slid open and Nicole was met by three pairs of eyes staring at her as if she had an extra eye in the middle of her forehead. Identical twin boys moved closer to their older sister, her arms going around their shoulders in a protective gesture.

"Are you going to be our new mother?" one boy asked. His expression was unfriendly, mirroring resentment.

Nicole's heart lurched and she glanced up at Zachary. He returned her stare, and Nicole recognized a deep brooding within Zachary for the first time.

"No, I'm not," she answered, reacting quickly. She had thought about a lot of things where it concerned Zachary Regan, but somehow becoming a mother to his children was not one of them. She refused to think that far in the future.

"Daddy, can I go to the mall with Kiani? We want to get our noses pierced," Zachary's daughter rattled off once the tense moment passed.

"Grandma wants to take us to Disney World on our winter recess," the other twin got out as soon as his sister inhaled.

All three children began talking at the same time and Zachary placed his forefingers in his mouth, whistling sharply. The high-pitched sound set off another round of frantic barking from Max.

"Where are your manners?" he reprimanded in a dangerously soft voice. "We have a guest."

"Sorry, Dad," all three chorused.

Zachary smiled. "That's better. Now, may Miss Moore and I come in?" He pointed a finger at Max, saying, "You, stay outside." Max whined and lowered his massive head.

"He's crying, Dad," Davy Regan moaned.

Zachary's hand went to the small of Nicole's back, directing her into a yawning entry that led to an enormous living room. Natural wood floors and walls abounded and she inhaled deeply, filling her lungs with their pungent fragrance.

"He's not crying," Zachary insisted.

Kathy watched her father help Nicole out of her coat. She took it and hung it up in a walk-in closet off the entry.

"Can...may I go to the mall, Daddy?"

"We'll talk about it later," Zachary answered.

Kathy's gaze shifted to Nicole and seeing her smile she returned it. At least her father hadn't said no.

Again Zachary's hand went to Nicole's waist. His fingers tightened possessively on her slim body. "Nicole, I'd like you to meet Katherine." His free arm curved around his daughter's shoulders. "Kathy, Miss Nicole Moore."

Kathy shyly extended her right hand. "Nice meeting you, Miss Moore."

Nicole smiled at Katherine Regan, grasping her fingers. She was her father's daughter. She'd inherited his rich, deep burnished brown coloring, black eyes and full mouth. Her exotic beauty was obvious, waiting to blossom with maturity.

"Thank you, Kathy."

David and Daniel Regan fidgeted, waiting to be introduced. They were mirror images of each other with coarse curling black hair and golden-brown eyes. Zachary released Kathy, extending his hand to his sons. "This young man is David." David stepped forward, and Zachary placed a large hand on his shoulder. He motioned to Danny. "And this young man is Daniel. Davy, Danny, Miss Nicole Moore."

"Nice meeting you," the two boys said as one.

"And it's my pleasure to meet you, Danny, Davy," Nicole returned with a friendly smile.

Introductions out of the way, Zachary dropped a kiss on the top of Kathy's head. "Please let Miss Hennie know that we'll have a guest for lunch."

Kathy pressed her head to Zachary's chest. "But, Daddy, can I go to the mall?" she pleaded softly.

"Go tell Miss Hennie, then we'll talk," Zachary replied quietly. Kathy rushed off to do her father's bidding.

"What about Grandma and Disney World?" Danny questioned, giving Zachary a narrowed glance.

A slight frown creased Zachary's forehead. "Your grandmother knows that we're going skiing during the recess."

Danny glanced at Davy for moral support. "But Dad, we can *always* go skiing."

"Right, Dad," Davy confirmed.

Zachary led Nicole into the living room, the two boys following closely. "And you can always go to Disney World. It's not going to close down next month. And you both know we have to take advantage of the weather for favorable ski conditions. You can go to Disney World for the Easter break or during the summer, while you can't ski in April or August."

"Dad!" Danny moaned.

Zachary seated Nicole on a pale yellow Italian leather love seat. Matching modular pieces were dwarfed in the spacious area. The mellowed gold and red tones of the wood walls and floor filled the space with brightness regardless of the time of day or the weather. She sat transfixed by the view from the towering arched windows, of sand dunes and the sea. A large colorfully-patterned dhurrie rug in yellow, red and orange added a delightful contrast.

There was the soft chiming of a telephone, but it ended after the first ring.

"Kathy!" Zachary, Danny and Davy confirmed with wide grins.

"She never lets it ring more than once," Danny complained.

"It's probably Kiani," Davy said. "All they ever want to do is go to the malls and look at boys."

Nicole hid her smile when Zachary said, "There's going to come a time when you guys will hang out at the malls to look at girls."

"Never!" Danny spat out.

"Not me," Davy added quickly.

Zachary winked at Nicole. "Sure, sure."

Kathy rushed back into the living room. "Daddy, Kiani's mother's leaving now. Can I go?"

He sighed heavily. "Yes—but no nose piercing."

Kathy managed a sorrowful look. "Please, Daddy."

"Holes in your ears are enough, Katherine Regan," Zachary replied in a firm tone. Kathy wore two sets of small gold hoops in each ear. "Forget about coming back here to sleep if you get a hole in your nose."

"Tell her, Dad," Danny urged.

Kathy shot her brother a lethal glare. "Chill out, little boy," she said between clenched teeth.

Zachary stood and reached into his trouser pocket. He deposited several bills into Kathy's outstretched palm. He withheld one, then at the last moment gave it to her.

Kathy rose on tiptoe, throwing her arms around his neck, and kissed his jaw. "Thanks, Daddy." She smiled at Nicole. "I'll see you later, Miss Moore."

"This is definitely not a democracy," Danny announced solemnly, staring at his sister's retreating back. "Kathy always gets what she wants and we don't."

"I agree," Davy stated, nodding.

Nicole wanted to laugh aloud when she registered Zachary's expression. His jaw dropped as he stared at his sons.

Crossing his arms over his chest, he glared down at Danny and Davy. "Is this an open insurrection or just a mild protest?"

Danny blinked several times and shifted his eyebrows. "This has nothing to do with rising from the dead, Dad."

Zachary folded his long frame down to the sofa. "I said insurrection, not resurrection. Insurrection means a revolt against an established order or government."

"Oh no, Dad," Davy returned softly. "We just want to talk about Grandma taking us to Disney World."

Removing his glasses, Zachary ran a hand over his face. "Your grandmother is well aware that she's not to make any plans for you until she speaks to me first." He lowered his hand, and his coal-black eyes were fixed on Danny, then Davy.

"I rearranged my work schedule to take you away, and we all agreed that we would spend that week skiing. Now you tell me that Grandma wants to take you to Disney World."

"And on The Big Red Boat," Davy reminded him.

"Oh yes, The Big Red Boat," Zachary whispered. "We can't forget that."

Danny, the more assertive of the twin boys, sat up straighter. "Well, Dad? What's it going to be? I told Grandma I'd call her back when you got home."

Zachary replaced his glasses. His jaw was tense.

"You can take Miss Moore skiing with you," Davy rationalized quickly when Zachary didn't reply.

Danny imitated his father when he crossed his arms over his chest. "That sounds good to me."

Nicole schooled her expression not to react to Davy's suggestion. Not only did she not want to ski, but she had no intention of going away with his father. As it was, she and Zachary saw too much of one another.

"I don't ski, Davy," she said quickly. "I don't like snow or cold weather."

"And you were out of line suggesting that, David Regan," Zachary chastised his son.

"But she doesn't have to ski, Dad," Davy insisted. "Miss Moore can keep you company so you won't miss us."

Zachary rose to his feet. "No more discussion. I'll call your grandmother."

Danny, now exhibiting less bravado, asked, "Does that mean we can go?"

Zachary mumbled a curse under his breath. Why was it he felt like an ogre? Since his in-laws had relocated to Florida they rarely saw their grandchildren. They were only asking for a week of their time.

"Yeah," he replied stiffly.

Both boys shot to their feet, giving each other high-fives. They were congratulating one another as they raced out of the living room and downstairs to the lower level.

Nicole stood up, smiling at Zachary. He stared down at her, then returned her smile. "I suppose you think I'm the biggest sucker coming and going."

She laid a hand on his arm. "Not at all." Her voice was low, seductive. "You're a wonderful father, Zack Regan."

"If you think I'm so wonderful, why don't you come away with me?" His words held a silky challenge.

Nicole felt her stomach muscles tighten. She wanted to do more than go away with Zachary Regan. She was in love with him and she wanted to share that love with him; and never had she ever wanted to belong to a man—totally.

"I can't." The refusal was ripped from her throat.

Zachary arched an eyebrow, his eyes fusing with hers. He visually measured the rapidly beating pulse in her delicate throat. What was she afraid of?

"The house has more than one bedroom," he teased with a dimpled grin.

"It's not the sleeping accommodations, Zachary," she retorted with a return of her normal spirit.

"Then what is it, Nikki?" he crooned.

Folding her hands on her hips, she gave him a saucy smile. "I just had a vacation."

"We can make it a long weekend."

Nicole placed a hand over his chest. "No, Zachary."

He captured her hand, bringing her fingers to his mouth. "We'll talk about it later."

She watched his lowered head, frowning. "I won't change my mind."

His chin came up slowly. "I think you will, Nikki."

A silent battle ensued, each challenging and measuring the other. Zachary wanted Nicole--all of her.

How wrong you are, Nicole thought. As long as she remained in control of her emotions she would continue to resist him. It wouldn't be easy, but she had to try.

The remainder of the morning and afternoon passed quickly for Nicole. She met Zachary's housekeeper, Henrietta Charles, and liked the woman immediately. A petite figure, smooth unlined face, sparkling dark eyes and glossy graying hair belied her claim as a senior citizen.

Miss Hennie, as she preferred to be called, was unable to conceal her surprise when Zachary introduced Nicole as a special friend. And once they were alone, Zachary confessed that he had never invited a single woman to his house.

Nicole digested this information while Zachary showed her about the converted carriage house. After seeing

Zachary's skills in redesigning the interior of Adam's home and his own, Nicole concluded that Zachary Regan had become an established artist in the conversion of older structures for living quarters.

He explained that he usually studied the history of the period, then converted the space where it would be comfortable and appealing while retaining the original spirit of the structure. His own house was no exception.

Arched windows, boldly contemporary, were layered with the carriage house's old elements for a play of contrasts. The bedrooms of the home were on the first floor, which allowed for the more public enjoyment of the light and views of the second floor. The expansive arched window at the back of the building and the small, intimate spaces inside were created by the sloping of the original walls and ceilings. Once the hayloft, the second floor held the kitchen, living and dining areas, and two guest spaces, all with a view of Long Island Sound. The entire effect was of outdoors—the grand slope of the ceiling and exposed rafters.

The beaded pine boards that had covered the stable ceilings now lined the walls of the entry and stair hall. These, and the area of original exposed brick and plank floors, were intriguingly rough next to the sleek, contemporary finish of the stair rail, the smooth cedar paneling of the upstairs ceiling, and the modern white of the house's exterior.

Nicole stood at the window in Zachary's studio, her hand on a powerful telescope, staring out at the whitecaps cresting the churning gray water as the brilliant winter sun dipped lower in the heavens.

Zachary moved behind her, his breath feathering across her neck. Both hands circled her waist. She leaned back, her head resting on his shoulder.

"It's been a wonderful day, Zachary. Thank you for inviting me."

He nuzzled her ear with his nose and curved his arms around her body. "I should be the one thanking you," he replied, his voice lowering to a sensual rasp. "I haven't felt like this in a long time."

Nicole shuddered and she was certain he felt it. "Like what?"

"Good."

"Good?" Nicole questioned.

Zachary rested his chin on the top of her head, smiling. "Yes, good."

"Just good?"

He turned her in his embrace. "Yes, good. How can I explain feeling good?"

She peered over his shoulder, noting the door to the studio was closed. Her arms slid up the expanse of his broad chest and curled around his neck. A mysterious smile softened her mouth. "Sometimes its better not to try explaining," she crooned softly.

"Then I'll have to show you," he returned, lowering his head. At the last moment, he removed his glasses and branded her mouth with a hot, searing kiss.

He kissed her hungrily, and Nicole returned his ardor with an unspoken hunger of her own. Her tongue outlined the shape of his mouth, and when he moaned through parted lips it slipped into his mouth.

The banked fires exploded. The chaste pecks on the lips and cheek over the past week were just a foil for the passion simmering beneath the surface.

Nicole's hands searched and slipped under the silky weave of his sweater, sweeping over his chest. Her fingers caught and were entwined in the thick, coarse hair on his body. Her fingertips grazed his male breasts, bringing the flat nipples into prominence.

Zachary groaned as if in pain. He was hurting. It had been weeks since he'd released his dammed passions, and it was only with Nicole did he want to share them. She had ruined him for any other woman.

He tore his mouth from hers, his gaze glazed and wild. "No...no. No more," he pleaded hoarsely. "We can't continue like this, Nicole."

Nicole tried slowing down her runaway heart. She nodded. Zachary was right. There was no way she could deny her love for him any more than one could ask the sun not to rise each morning.

"You're right, Zachary," she confirmed, eyes closed and her trembling breasts rising and falling heavily. "Please take me home."

That wasn't what he meant. "Nikki..."

"Now, Zachary," she implored, interrupting him.

He replaced his glasses and walked over to the door. Opening it, he waited for her to proceed him out of the room.

Nicole was saved from making her farewell known to the others when she realized that she and Zachary were alone in the house. Miss Hennie had gone to the store, Danny and Davy to their friend's house, while Kathy hadn't returned from the mall.

The trip from Oyster Bay to Manhattan was accomplished in complete silence. Zachary ignored Nicole's protest when she said she didn't need him to see her to her door. He held her arm in a tight grip as he led her down the hall to her apartment.

She turned to face him and thank him again, but was thwarted when he pulled her up close. This time there was no hint of passion in his kiss. His frustration overrode his anger when he bruised her mouth in a punishing kiss. She felt the bite of his fingers through the thick fabric of her pea jacket and the outline of the buckle on the belt circling his waist.

Nicole felt her teeth against the tender flesh of her lower lip before she tasted blood. She struggled to free herself. "No," she moaned. "Please, Zack," she pleaded.

Zachary registered her plaintive plea and somewhere, somehow, in the fog of frustration and fear his anger fled. Burying his face in her neck, he breathed a kiss there, under her ear and back to her bruised mouth.

Large, unshed tears filled her golden eyes and he felt his chest tighten. "I'm sorry, Nikki," he crooned close to her trembling mouth. He inhaled her sweet feminine scent. "I love you too much to hurt you."

In the second it took for Nicole to register his unexpected confession, Zachary had turned and was striding down the length of the hall to the elevator.

Nicole could barely see how to fit her key in the lock when the tears threatened to overflow. She opened the door and Vera met her in the entry. Nicole's tortured expression spoke volumes.

Vera held out her arms, but Nicole disappointed her when she brushed past her. But Vera was not daunted. "I want you to get undressed, get into bed and I'll bring you something hot to drink. Then we'll talk."

Nicole didn't want to talk; she wanted to scream, cry, throw things. But she complied with Vera's request, slipping out of her jacket and heading for the bedroom.

Dressed in a sweatsuit, Nicole pressed her back against the massive headboard and cradled the snowy-white bear to her chest. She'd managed not to cry, swallowing back her pain, however her head throbbed relentlessly.

"You love him?" Vera asked with a direct look. Nicole nodded and clutched the bear tighter. "How much?"

Nicole sighed. "A lot."

"Enough to marry him and have his children?" Vera questioned incredulously.

"Yes," she sighed again.

Vera bit down on her lower lip. "This is serious, Nick."

Nicole closed her eyes, trying to will away her headache. "Very serious," she mumbled.

"Does he love you?" Vera continued with her questioning.

Nicole repeated what Zachary had said about loving and hurting her.

"He's telling you that he loves you, Nick."

She reopened her eyes, shaking her head. "That's not what he meant at all, Vera."

"But he said..."

"I know what he said. He didn't say 'I love you, Nicole'. What he meant was that I had nothing to fear from him because he loves me. It's the same kind of love I have for you as a friend."

Vera wasn't convinced. "I don't think so."

Nicole moaned and sank down to the pile of pillows cradling her back. "I can't think anymore. My head is pounding."

Vera left the bed. "I'll get you a couple of aspirins. After you relax we'll decide what we're going to do for the rest of the weekend."

Nicole swallowed the two aspirins and within half an hour she was asleep. It was eight-thirty when she awoke to the sound of the telephone. It was Carson inviting her out to a club where a friend of his was appearing in a stand-up comedy act. She wanted to plead fatigue, but decided to accept. She needed the company of another man, any man, to keep her from thinking about Zachary Regan.

Carson's friend was quite talented, and she found herself laughing uncontrollably at his real event jokes, interspersed with racy overtones. It was what she needed to dispel her dark mood.

She and Carson walked from the club back to his loft apartment and spent hours laughing and trying to remember the jokes told by the more than six young comedians trying to break into the business.

It was after two when Carson left her at her apartment. Vera was still up, watching a classic Bogart film. Vera gave Carson a perfunctory salute, then turned her attention back to the television screen.

Vera waited until Carson left and Nicole sat down beside her on the love seat, then said, "Zachary Regan called less than ten minutes after you'd left. I told him that you were out on a date." She managed a quick glance at Nicole's expressionless face. "He said there was no message. I must admit that he's good, Nick. The inflection in his voice never changed. He may be talented and gorgeous, but I don't envy you, Nick. He's controlled; perhaps too controlled; he's even better than you are," she added.

Nicole smiled, nodding. "I think you're right, Vera."

"What are you going to do about it?"

"Count my losses and retreat."

Vera ignored the flickering images on the screen, peering at Nicole. "You're serious, aren't you?"

"Very serious." She gave Vera a brittle smile. "It's

too bad Zachary Regan doesn't know how serious I am.''

And she was serious. She didn't return Zachary's call the following day and she managed to push him to the farthest recesses of her mind until Monday. He left a message with the receptionist that she return his call. But even if Nicole considered returning the call she couldn't. She was still covering for the social worker with the broken ankle, which meant she had to complete her own administrative responsibilities and handle a caseload of more than thirty clients; all of the clients were Spanish-speaking cases.

The late-night receptionist-secretary slipped Nicole a note while she gulped down a container of lukewarm coffee and a half-eaten wilted salad. She scanned the note quickly and stood up, discarding the tasteless meal in a plastic bag and depositing it in a wastebasket.

Zachary had decided to come to the center. He was waiting for her. He registered her fatigue immediately when she stepped into the reception area. There was a slight puffiness under her eyes and a tightness around her mouth.

A small hand touched her arm. ''Dr. Moore.''

''*Un momento, por favor,*'' Nicole said, smiling at the woman who looked much younger than her eighteen years. She nodded at Zachary and motioned for him to come away from the dozen people sitting on the metal folding chairs. All eyes were trained on the tall man and woman standing close together.

''Yes, Zachary.'' Her voice was a low monotone.

He yearned to touch her, hold her close, but didn't. He didn't want to embarrass her or himself.

"What time do you expect to get off?"

Nicole sighed and her shoulders dropped slightly. "I don't know. We usually close at nine, but tonight we're backed up. I'm covering for someone out on disability."

"I'll wait for you."

"That's not necessary." Her tone was flat.

Zachary shrugged out of his topcoat. "I said I'll wait."

Nicole turned and made her way to the young woman. She couldn't argue with Zachary. Not in front of the clients.

Nicole felt a shiver of relief. Zachary coming to her would make it easy; easy for her to end their relationship.

Chapter Ten

"What can I do, Dr. Moore?"

Nicole leaned back in her chair, staring at Milagros Gomez's tear-stained face. "You can move out," she stated quietly.

"But...but he won't let me."

Nicole braced her elbows on the arms of her chair and leaned forward. "And why can't you, Millie? You're eighteen, you work, you're emancipated."

Millie's shoulders shook as she sobbed quietly in her cupped hands. Nicole waited for her crying to subside.

"I'm not afraid for myself, Dr. Moore. I'm afraid of what my father will do to Ricky."

"Has he threatened to harm your boyfriend?"

Millie blew her nose in a shredded tissue. Her large dark brown eyes were red from weeping and filled with more pain than a young adult was expected to undergo.

"No. I think it's only because Ricky is a cop."

Nicole schooled her expression not to reveal the anger she felt for the elder Gomez. Millie and her parents were seen in group family counseling sessions, yet after two years Manuel Gomez had not relinquished his dominating hold on his wife and daughter.

"Is Ricky willing to help you?"

Millie managed a sad smile. "He wants to marry me."

Nicole arched an eyebrow and smiled. "Have you accepted?" Millie shook her head. "Why not?"

The young woman flushed a deep color. She ran a slender hand through the wealth of naturally curly black hair falling over her forehead.

"I'm not ready to sleep with him."

"Do you love him?"

A dreamy smile softened Millie's lush mouth. "Very much."

"Have you verbalized to Ricky that you're not ready to sleep with him?"

Her flush deepened. "No," she replied softly. "It's not as if he hasn't tried, but I just tell him no."

"You have three options, Milagros."

Millie stared at Nicole. The only time Dr. Moore called her Milagros was when she lectured her.

"The first one," Nicole continued smoothly, "is to remain at home and pray that your father will change. We both know that's not likely to happen in the very near future. The second option is to ask Ricky to help you financially if you don't have enough money saved to secure an apartment. Or either you could accept Ricky's offer of marriage, where he'd offer you his love and protection. Whatever you decide, I suggest you let Ricky know that you're not ready to sleep with him. I'm willing to bet the man's not a mind reader."

Millie laughed, transforming her delicate features and erasing her unhappiness. "Do you think he'll understand?"

Nicole offered her own smile. "If he truly loves you — yes." She glanced at the clock on the desk. "Our time is up, Millie. I still have to see two others before I can go home."

Millie stood, a tortured frown wrinkling her forehead. "Can I see you next week, Dr. Moore? I know Mrs. Rivera will be back, but I prefer seeing you."

"Let me talk it over with Mrs. Rivera," Nicole said noncommittally.

"Good night, and thank you, Dr. Moore."

"Good night, Millie."

Nicole waited for Millie to leave, then opened a file. She jotted down her observations and recommendations on a legal pad. She would have to take the notes home and write them up before handing them in to the typist in the morning. It was the only part of casework she detested— the endless report writing.

Nicole saw two more clients, and it was nearly ten when she slipped her notes into a large tote and flipped off the light in the office.

Becoming involved with Maria Rivera's clients had temporarily dismissed the fact that Zachary Regan was waiting for her. Nicole entered the reception area and came up short. The large space was empty except for Zachary and Irene Williams.

Nicole was shocked with the scene. The center's head psychologist was smiling up at him, a dreamy expression on her beautiful face. Zachary appeared equally charmed. His stance—arms crossed over his broad chest as he leaned down to hear what Irene was saying—indicated supreme male arrogance and cockiness.

Nicole's breath caught in her chest when she visually appraised the cut of his dark gray suit with a double-breasted jacket. It was the suit he'd worn the first night she met him. His cashmere topcoat was thrown over the back of a chair and she remembered the luxurious feel of the pile and the distinctive fragrance of his after-shave that clung to the fibers.

She didn't know why, but she knew what Zachary Regan looked like and smelled like with her eyes closed. Everything that was him had unconsciously seeped into her being. The feel of the flesh covering his smooth jaw, the thick coarse curl of his hair and the strength in his muscular body.

I want him.

And she did. She didn't want to send him away; she didn't want to wake up in the morning and know that she couldn't call him; wouldn't see him. And she didn't understand why she was so ambivalent where it concerned Zachary Regan.

I love him. I hate him. I want him. I don't want him.

He was making her crazy. If this was what it meant to be in love, she wanted no part of it.

She moved slightly and the motion was enough to capture Zachary's attention. Turning his head slowly, he stared at her.

Irene also turned, and a smile was slow in coming. "I'm ready to lock it up," she informed Nicole.

Nicole hoisted her tote to her shoulder and made her way towards the door. She complimented herself for successfully concealing her uneasiness when seeing Zachary with Irene. There was no way she would add to his arrogance by letting him know she was jealous.

"Where are you parked, Irene?"

Irene tapped the large earring in her right ear with a forefinger. "I have a spot right out front."

Nicole continued to ignore Zachary. "Good night. I'll

see you in the morning," she said to Irene.

Irene pursed her mouth, expecting Nicole to introduce her to Zachary. When she didn't, she shrugged her shoulders and mumbled a soft good night under her breath.

Zachary slipped on his topcoat and followed Nicole out into the cold, winter night. He caught her arm and pulled her close to his side.

"What happened to your manners, Dr. Moore?"

Nicole didn't slow her brisk stride. Staring straight ahead, she said, "I don't know what you're talking about." Her warm breath was frothy in the frigid air.

"You didn't introduce me to your colleague." He tightened his hold on her arm and both of them raced across the wide avenue before the light changed.

"You didn't look as if you needed an introduction, Zachary. You and Irene looked cozy enough without my intervention."

His arm slipped down to her waist. Lowering his head, his mouth grazed the mass of curls dancing around her face. "You sound jealous, darling."

"You wish, buddy," she snorted.

"I know, Nikki."

"You know nothing, Zachary Regan."

"I know enough," he chuckled.

She pushed against his shoulder. "Get away from me!"

"I think the lady protests too much."

They made their way down to Second Avenue. The streets and sidewalks were deserted. It was late, cold and dark, and that meant most people were indoors escaping the blasts of arctic air sweeping down from Canada.

"Where's your car?" Nicole asked Zachary as they neared her apartment complex.

"I found a space near your building. It's a homing

pigeon. Turn it on and it winds up here."

"Real cute," she sneered.

"I'll excuse your bad mood because I know you've worked late," Zachary countered in the dangerously soft tone Nicole had come to recognize, knowing he was holding his temper in check. "But if you didn't burn the candle at both ends, then you'd have enough strength to sustain you for your late nights."

"What's that supposed to mean?" she questioned, rounding on him.

"You can't date me and other men at the same time, Nicole."

She stopped at the entrance to her building, staring up at him. "You don't own me, Zachary Regan."

A muscle flicked angrily in his jaw as his mouth twisted wryly. "You're right about that, Nicole," he returned, so quietly that she had to strain to hear his words. "I don't own you but I do love you."

Her eyes froze on his lips, not believing him. "You...you...I..."

Zachary smiled a sexy dimpled smile. Taking her gloved hand in his, he led her into the building. They both nodded at the doorman, returning his greeting, the words sounding stilted and foreign.

Nicole's hands were shaking when she retrieved her mail from the mailbox while Zachary waited at the elevators. She pushed the letters and magazines into her tote and joined Zachary at the elevators.

She thought maybe she had imagined his words, but seeing the soft caress of his black eyes Nicole knew she had heard correctly.

The elevator arrived and Nicole walked in, pressing her back against one wall while Zachary stood against the opposite one. It was as if they didn't trust one another's closeness. Their gazes fused and locked during the rapid ascent.

Nicole didn't remember walking the hall or handing Zachary the keys to unlock the door to her apartment. She didn't remember him removing her coat and hanging it up in the closet. Nor did she remember him leading her into the living room, settling her on the love seat or handing her a glass of chilled white wine.

But she did remember being cradled in his arms and watching the winking lights of the bridges spanning the East River from the expanse of glass running the length of the living and dining areas.

"I love you, Nicole," Zachary whispered in her ear, eliciting a shiver of wanting from her.

She closed her eyes and buried her face in his strong throat. "Zachary, I..."

"Hush, sweetheart," he crooned. You don't have to say anything. Not now. I just want you to know how I feel. I'm not asking you to love me. Just don't send me away."

Pulling back, Nicole stared up at him in the darkness. 'I'm not going to send you away."

"Not now. But you were going to, weren't you?"

She relaxed against his body, pressing her mouth to his chin. Her moist mouth tasted his skin. Her fingers replaced her tongue, grazing the emerging hairs of a beard.

Zachary laughed deep in his chest. "What are you doing?"

Nicole moaned sensuously. "Tasting you."

"How do I taste?" He drained his glass and placed it on the carpeted floor.

Her tongue flicked over his chin. "Good. Very, very good."

"Were you going to send me away, Nicole?"

She swore to herself. Zachary Regan had a mind like a steel trap. It didn't let anything escape.

His fingers caught in her hair, massaging her scalp; the soothing gesture sent electric shocks through her. "Were you?"

Nicole refused to answer him as her right hand slipped in the opening where Zachary had removed his tie and undid the first two buttons on his shirt. She caressed muscle, flesh and hair.

Zachary caught her wrist, pulling her hand away from his bare chest. "Answer me, Nicole."

"Yes! Yes, yes, yes. I was going to stop seeing you," she admitted, her temper flaring. "I didn't know where I stood with you from one day to the next. From the very beginning it was 'I don't want to get involved, Nicole; I don't intend to get married again; there's no room in my life for a woman.' How did you expect me to react, Zachary?"

She pulled out of his grip and walked over to the window. Wrapping her arms around her body in a protective gesture, she closed her eyes.

"I didn't want to get involved either," she confessed. "I knew I'd be courting heartache. One day I loved you, then I hated you the next. I was on a seesaw, a roller coaster and a carousel with you, Zachary. Up and down, round and round." Turning, she faced him. "That's what I've been going through for the past few weeks. And I don't like it."

Zachary left the love seat and walked over to her. Taking her hands in his, he placed them on his chest, holding them in place.

"I know I haven't made it easy for you, darling. That's because it hasn't been easy for me. I'm not asking you to love me, but I do want you to trust me."

"But I do..."

"Don't, Nikki. Don't tell me what you think I want to hear." He placed a finger over her mouth. "Please give me time to work something out."

Nicole felt the ravages of frustration in her chest. She loved him and he didn't want her love. What did he want?

"How much time, Zachary?"

He registered her skepticism. "I don't know. I can't erase overnight what has been festering for six years."

A warning voice whispered in her head. Six years. It had something to do with his late wife. Had he in some way contributed to her death?

She chose her words carefully. "Okay, Zachary. I'll give you all the time you need."

He cradled her head between his hands. "Thank you," he whispered against her lips.

Suddenly Nicole felt the urge to be alone to sort out her new feelings and fear. She pushed gently against his chest and he released her.

Zachary flashed a half-smile. "I'd better go and let you get some sleep."

"Yes," she breathed out nervously.

The light from the kitchen provided Zachary with enough illumination when he gathered his tie and suit jacket. Nicole stood quietly, silently, watching him put on his topcoat. She managed a sad smile when he curved a hand under her chin and kissed her mouth.

"I'm going to Chicago in the morning to see my aunt," he informed her. "She hasn't been feeling well, and I want to make certain she receives the proper medical care."

Nicole nodded. "When will you return?"

"Thursday. I don't want to miss our Valentine's Day

celebration," he said with a wide grin.

Her love for him overshadowed any doubts and fears that she felt when she put her arms around his neck. "I'll be waiting for you."

Zachary crushed her to his body, committing everything about her to memory. It had to be enough until he returned. At last, reluctantly, they parted, then he turned and walked out of the apartment.

All thoughts of rewriting her notes faded quickly. She would get up early in the morning and complete it.

Nicole didn't know why she couldn't summon the joy she should've felt when Zachary told her that he loved her. It was as if he was forced to tell her because he was afraid of losing her. But lose her to whom? Certainly not Carson.

Was he jealous of her seeing Carson? Why not, she thought. She had certainly felt her own pangs of the green monster when she saw him talking to Irene.

But one could only feel jealous when one cared. And she cared for him; she loved him. But why was it she didn't feel secure knowing Zachary loved her? He may have loved her, but was it a different kind of love than the one he had had with the mother of his children?

He'd asked for time. And she would give him that time. Nicole sighed heavily and smiled. She had waited thirty-three years for the right man. A few more months or maybe even a year would be worth it if that man was Zachary Regan.

Irene extended her coffee mug to Nicole. "Why is it that we can't stay away from this place?" she teased with a tired smile.

Nicole smiled at Irene over her shoulder. "That's

because we're *enferma en la cabeza."*

"*Cabeza* I understand," Irene countered. She took the mug Nicole had filled with coffee. The limited space in the employee snack area had only enough room for two, very slim, persons at one time. "I really should take some classes to learn to speak Spanish."

Nicole added a dollop of milk to her own coffee. "We could use some help. Then you'd be the additional backup whenever we don't have a Spanish-speaking therapist."

Irene compressed her lips, giving Nicole a penetrating look. "How are you feeling?"

"Fine."

"Even though you're putting in ten-hour days?"

Nicole leaned a hip against the counter and took a sip of coffee. She peered at Irene over the rim. "It's only until Maria gets back."

"Are you going to take some time off?"

Now Nicole's curiosity was piqued. Why was Irene concerned about her physical well-being?

"We have the long President's Day weekend," she replied cautiously. "I can extend that by a day or two."

"Would you resent some professional advice, Dr. Moore?" Irene questioned.

Nicole shrugged her shoulders. "Not at all, Dr. Williams."

"Take the time off and enjoy yourself." She adjusted the challis shawl over her shoulder and left the snack area.

Nicole lowered her mug slowly to the countertop. What did Irene mean? And what had she said to Zachary? More importantly, what had he said to Irene? And Nicole did not feel comfortable knowing they had probably discussed her.

She picked up her cup and made her way back to her office when one of the social workers stumbled blindly towards the coffee maker.

She sat down at her desk, staring at the stack of mail in the wire basket. Her eyes narrowed when she remembered Zachary warning her about burning the candle at both ends. But then he was talking about her social life—dating him and dating Carson.

How she wished he was still in New York where she could confront him. It would have to wait until he returned from Chicago.

The day sped by quickly and Nicole considered herself blessed when she left the center at six-thirty. She picked up her dinner at a popular Chinese take-out restaurant and went home to do several loads of laundry, then relax.

The next day was another late night and when Nicole returned home she barely made it through her nightly ritual, falling asleep as soon as her head touched the pillow.

The sharp ringing of the telephone pulled Nicole out of a deep sleep early the following morning.

"Yes," she mumbled into the receiver.

"Nicole, it's Joe."

She came awake immediately when she heard her boss's voice. "What's up, Joe?"

"Did you look out of the window?"

Nicole pulled herself up on an elbow and peered through the lacy panels covering her bedroom window. There was a shield of bright gray.

"It's snowing," she stated flatly.

"It's a blizzard, Nicole. I'm closing the center."

Nicole sat up, cradling the receiver under her chin. "How much snow?"

"A lot. It started sometime after midnight and it hasn't

let up. The weather people are predicting at least a foot or more before it ends."

Nicole searched her memory for Irene's number. The snow emergency plan was set up as a telephone chain. Joe Nash called her and she called Irene.

"I'll call Irene, then she'll call the next person on the list," Nicole reported to Joe.

"Nicole?"

"Yes, Joe."

"Happy Valentine's Day."

She managed a smile. "Same to you." She pressed the button and dialed Irene's number.

Three minutes later she snuggled back down under the fluffy quilt, thinking about Zachary. He was scheduled to return to New York that morning.

Thinking of Zachary prompted her to reach for the T.V. remote. She switched on the television and pressed the button for the weather channel. Adjusting the sheet and blanket, she settled back and watched the screen.

She stared intently at the reports of blizzard conditions for the northeast. The dark green and bright red areas on the map spread from Virginia through Maine. There were images of stranded cars, trucks and slow-moving snow plows trying to clear blocked roads and streets.

Print across the lower portion of the screen reported that all three of the major airports were closed. Incoming and outgoing air traffic had come to a standstill.

Between cups of coffee and telephone calls from Vera and to her parents, Nicole watched the televised weather reports. The snowfall was predicted to equal or exceed the storms of '69 and '78.

She spent most of the morning prowling around the apartment like a restless cat or staring out of the window.

She wasn't used to the inactivity.

Nicole flicked off the T.V. and turned on the radio. She had been saturated with the weather reports, which were now the major headline news.

Reclining on the living room floor, a pillow cradled under her head, Nicole closed her eyes and listened to the tape of old songs. She smiled when hearing Roberta Flack and Donny Hathaway's *"The Closer I Get To You."* The words conjured up the scene where she had shared a dance with Zachary. The sensual images that followed brought a hot flush to her body. It was the first time Zachary had kissed her. A kiss that was so different from the one he'd stolen in his car before he left for Texas. All of it seemed so long ago; so many things had happened in the past few weeks.

The buzz of the intercom jolted her back to reality. She pushed gracefully to her feet and moved over to press the button. "Yes?"

"Mr. Regan," came the doorman's announcement.

"Please let him in." NIcole could barely hear her own voice over the rapid beating of her heart. He had come back. But when—how?

She didn't have long to wait for answers when she opened the door to his knock.

Zachary dropped his bags to the floor and gathered her tightly to his chest. "Happy Valentine's Day, darling," he whispered before taking her mouth in a hot, possessive kiss.

Nicole felt the scrape of stiff whiskers against her tender jaw, but she didn't care. All that mattered was that Zachary was there. She could touch him, smell him and taste his drugging moist mouth.

"When did yu get in?" she asked once he released her and picked up his luggage.

"The plane arrived in New York about seven, but we couldn't land at LaGuardia. It finally touched down at Newark, and I had to bribe a car service to drive me across the George Washington Bridge. Once in Manhattan, I must have tried a half dozen automatic teller machines to get enough cash to bribe New York City cabbies to bring me across town."

He removed his glasses and Nicole helped him out of his coat. "One dropped me at One Hundred and Forty-Ninth and Third Avenue. He was on his way back to the depot. It took the next driver almost two hours to drive two miles."

Nicole shook out the moisture from his coat, then hung it up in the closet. Zachary hadn't shaved and he looked tired.

"May I use your telephone to call home?"

Nicole's gaze was caressing and loving. "Of course. *Mi casa, su casa.*"

Zachary kissed her forehead, a hand catching in the tousled curls falling on her neck. "You may live to regret those words."

"Never," she breathed out against his lips.

He gave her a smoldering look. "Then you're stuck with a guest until this storm breaks. I'm staying, Nikki."

The enormity of their situation assailed her. She and Zachary were thrown together by forces beyond their control—the weather.

"How about something hot to drink?" she asked smoothly.

Zachary wasn't put off by her impassive expression. His eyes shifted to the throbbing pulse in her throat. "After I shave and shower," he replied in a quiet tone.

Nicole was left standing in the entry while Zachary headed for the phone on the wall in the dining area. She had planned for an intimate Valentine's Day celebration; and it looked as if that was what it was going to be.

Chapter Eleven

Zachary emerged from the bathroom, his jaw smooth and his healthy brown skin glistening from moisture. Barefoot, and wearing a pair of faded jeans and a T-shirt, he exemplified the quintessential male: tall, dark and handsome.

Tilting his chin, he sniffed the air like a big cat. "Do I smell food?" A wide grin split his face. "You're cooking! I can't believe you're actually cooking."

Nicole folded her hands on her hips. "Don't get wise, Zachary," she threatened. "I'm only heating up something I bought from the store."

Zachary shook his head in amazement and walked into the small kitchen and lifted the lid from a saucepan. A billow of steam emitted a savory aroma.

"What is it?" He replaced the lid.

"Lobster bisque," Nicole replied as she opened the refrigerator door. "I've put together a salad, but you can have the honor of preparing the dressing."

Zachary moved behind Nicole, closed the door and wound his arms around her middle. "What else do you want me to do, darling?"

Nicole glanced up at him over her shoulder. "Warm up the bread."

He kissed the side of her neck. "I knew there would be a catch," he murmured along the column of her throat.

"What do you say to a picnic?"

"In the snow?" he asked, still raining kisses on her throat.

Nicole turned in his loose embrace and smiled up at him. "No. On the living room floor. I'll try anything to conjure up summer."

Zachary stared down into her gold-flecked eyes. There was a carefree light he had never seen before. Everything about Nicole appeared serene and ethereal. She wore the look of a woman in love. Could he hope that she loved him as much as he loved her.

"You're on." He dropped a kiss on the end of her nose.

Nicole rose on tiptoe and touched her lips to his smiling mouth. His arms tightened around her waist and he drank from the lush sweetness of her soft lips. The kiss lingered, as he tasted the flowing nectar she so willingly offered. Both of them were breathing heavily when they parted.

"I'd better set up the picnic table," Nicole said, running her tongue over her lower lip.

Zachary nodded, staring numbly at her. This kiss was different; it was deep and profound, exhibiting none of the frantic passion that usually flowed between them.

He was almost willing to hope—hope that his fear was fading. That he could love Nicole—unselfishly and with the promise that he could share his life with her; a life free of nightmares of his loving and losing.

Nicole felt his gaze on her back even after she'd turned and walked into the living room. She felt an undercurrent of uneasiness that had nothing to do with the intimacy of their situation. She and Zachary were trapped, but this trap was one without visible bounds. Despite his protests they were drawn together as if destiny had willed it.

She would not fight fate, for if the forces willed it, then she and Zachary Regan would have more than memories.

Nicole searched the armoire for a small tablecloth. Within minutes she had set the coffee table with china, silver and a pair of scented candles. Several fat cushions were pulled from the love seat onto the floor for seating.

She surveyed her handiwork, smiling. At the last moment she added a small flowering potted plant as a centerpiece.

"Your cupboards are quite interesting, Nikki," Zachary called out from the kitchen.

Nicole returned to the kitchen to find Zachary examining a rack filled with exotic spices. "That was a gift," she explained.

He turned and smiled. "I think someone is trying to give you a hint, sweetheart."

She felt her cheeks heat up. "No, Zachary. I'm not going to learn to cook."

He replaced the spices, holding out a hand to her. "Come here."

The two words tumbled from his lips like watered silk. The heat from her face spread downward, searing all of the secret places.

Moving towards him trance-like, Nicole floated into his embrace. She wound her arms around his solid middle and inhaled the very essence that was Zachary Regan.

Zachary rested his chin on the top of her head and closed his eyes. "You don't ever have to learn to cook. I love you the way you are.

"I hear a voice inside of me that sometimes cries out through all of the uncertainty," he continued in the quiet voice that Nicole savored. "With you there is so much uncertainty and I want answers; answers to why I've fallen in love with you; answers to why it's taken so many years to realize my fears."

Nicole sensed his disquiet. "What fears, Zachary?"

Zachary pulled back and stared down at her trusting face. "The fear that I'm going to lose you."

A slight frown creased her forehead. "I love you, Zachary. I'm not going anywhere."

"I'm not talking about you going away."

She hesitated, trying to analyze what Zachary had just revealed. *Be objective, Nicole,* she thought. *Think of him as a client.*

"Do you want to tell me of your fears?" she asked in a soft, urging tone.

Zachary ran a sculpted hand over his face, dropping it slowly to his side. "I don't know if I can," he admitted.

"Because I'm a part of your fears?" He nodded. "Do you want me to recommend someone else you can talk to?"

His jaw clenched and his eyes narrowed slightly. "No. This is something I have to work out myself."

Nicole exhibited an ease she didn't necessarily feel. She cradled his face between her hands, exalting in the feel of smooth firm brown flesh warming her palms. "Do you think it would be better if we didn't see one another until you work through your problem?"

Zachary imprisoned her wrists with long fingers. "No!" His eyes flickered wildly.

Nicole's mind raced quickly.. She had to give Zachary the space he needed to be objective. "Darling, I love you. And because I do, I'll be here for you—now and forever."

Zachary eased his hold on the fragile bones of her wrists and a sad smile touched his lips. "Call it faith, but something tells me to believe in you."

She took a step and laid her head against his shoulder. "Believe it, Zachary."

He held her tightly in a bone-crushing grip. "How will I make it not seeing you? Not hearing your voice? Not tasting your sweet mouth?"

"Do you think it's going to be easy for me, too?"

"You have your boyfriends."

"I don't have any boyfriends, Zachary," Nicole protested softly.

"Men friends, or whatever the hell they are to you."

Nicole smiled, raising her chin. "Jealousy isn't an admirable trait, Zachary."

"Neither is celibacy," he shot back softly with a dimpled grin.

"A little denial is good for the soul."

"Any more denial will turn me into a real sexual deviant," he hissed, wiggling his eyebrows.

Nicole wasn't as amused. "Sleeping together will only complicate everything."

Zachary sobered, exhaling heavily. "I know that. But I've never entertained the notion of becoming a monk."

She rose on tiptoe and kissed his pouting mouth. "It'll be over soon."

"I know, darling. I believe in you," he whispered hoarsely and returned her kiss with his vow. And knowing there would be no further intimacy, Nicole and Zachary began a gentle exploration of the other's body, committing curves and planes to memory.

The snow continued to fall against an icy whitened sky as the howl of the wind reverberated against the windows, swirling the flakes in dizzying patterns. The warmth and laughter inside the apartment belied the fury of the winter storm.

Nicole cradled her back against a pile of throw pillows while Zachary anchored his head on a fist, supported by an elbow. Both of them wore the look of sated lovers.

Zachary's lids lowered over his fathomless black eyes. "The picnic was a wonderful idea, Nikki."

Closing her own eyes, Nicole rested her head on several pillows and smiled. "Thank you."

He shifted, moving closer to her on the floor. "We must do this again."

"When?" she questioned, not opening her eyes.

Zachary pulled his legs out from under the coffee table and looped them over Nicole's, making her his prisoner. "Soon," he crooned quietly against her ear. "Very soon."

Her lids fluttered open. Zachary's face was mere inches from her own and her gaze caressed his face gently, lovingly.

She wanted to belong to him—totally; and at that moment never had Nicole wanted more to be married.

His lush lips brushed hers. "I never realized you would become so special to me," he confessed, tasting her pliant mouth.

"How special?" she asked softly.

Zachary released her and rose fluidly to his feet. "Wait here and I'll show you."

Nicole's eyes crinkled in amusement when she watched Zachary retreat to the bedroom. Minutes later he returned and dropped a small gift-wrapped package in her lap.

He hunkered down next to her and pressed a kiss to her forehead. "Happy Valentine's Day, darling."

Nicole was inordinately slow in peeling off the gold bow, tape and gold foil paper. Her heart began a loud pounding when she stared down at the small velvet box cradled in the palm of her hand.

Thick lashes concealed her gaze from Zachary when he stared at her face. Her well-groomed fingers lingered over the velvet surface, then tightened and opened the cover.

Nicole closed her eyes briefly, trying to bring her fragile emotions under control. Zachary's gift was an exquisite large diamond heart suspended from a platinum chain.

A knowing smile deepened the dimple in Zachary's cheek. "I'm giving you my heart to keep, Nikki," he crooned. He took the pendant from her and secured it around her slender neck.

Nicole laid a hand over the brilliant stones. "I suppose this makes me my love's keeper," she said quietly.

"Yes, it does," Zachary confirmed, easing her down to the pillows and covering her body with his. "Oh yes it does, darling," he confirmed, holding her close to his heart.

* * * * * * * * * *

Nicole closed her eyes, still seeing the blooming dogwood trees lining Adam's driveway. Fragile petals littered the thick carpet of grass like confetti.

"Tired, baby sister?"

Nicole shook her head, then reopened her eyes. Adam's dark green eyes crinkled when he smiled down at her.

"Just relaxing."

Adam leaned over and kissed her forehead. "I'll leave you to your relaxing."

"Where are you going?"

Adam Moore jangled a set of keys in his hand. "I have to drop some papers off to a client."

Nicole shifted an arching eyebrow. "When did you start working weekends?"

"This is a *special* client."

Nicole laughed. "Who is she?"

Adam ruffled her hair. "Careful, honey, you're beginning to sound like Mama." Turning, he walked down the porch steps towards the sports car parked in the circular drive.

Nicole leaned forward in the rocker. "I'm going to haunt you, Adam Moore, until you tell me," she teased.

Adam thumbed his nose at her when he slipped behind the wheel. Moments later his car's taillights disappeared completely in the waning daylight.

Nicole stared out into the encroaching darkness and began rocking. She found it hard to believe that she could feel peace; a warm, soothing, comforting peace even though she had not seen Zachary for nearly two and a half months; and despite not speaking and seeing one another, they still managed to communicate.

Zachary had left her apartment the morning after the Valentine's Day snow storm, promising to seek the help he needed to conquer the fear that had held him captive for years. Nicole felt as if she was losing a piece of herself when he walked her to the family center, then turned and left her staring at his broad back.

A week later, a messenger delivered a stuffed animal—this one a bear wearing a Chicago Bulls scarf and hat. After that flowers were delivered with such regularity that her office began to resemble a florist.

Nicole treasured his gifts and reciprocated with mementos of the New York Mets, Yankees, Rangers, Islanders and Knicks. Her geocentric counterattack signaled an all out barrage from Zachary. He sent her terse one-word notes with accompanying caricatures reading: milksop, coward and ungrateful.

Each time she dissolved in a spasm of laughter, then retaliated with her own delicately scented notes bearing: wimp, dork and insidious.

The flowers, stuffed toys and notes were enough to raise her spirits above the self-pitying level. Her responsibilities at the center kept her busy, while she managed to find time to attend the health club with Vera, visit several antique shops along fashionable Madison Avenue, attend an auction at Sothby's and attend several board meetings for neighborhood organizations.

Spring had put in an early appearance, buoying her spirits when she awoke each morning to find the young trees putting forth fat, ripe buds.

However, Virginia had bypassed spring and embraced summer by the time she arrived in Virginia for her parents' forty-fifth wedding anniversary celebration. She and Adam, with their father's intervention, had planned a small dinner party at Adam's house for Jonathan and Margaret and presented them with tickets for a twenty-one day cruise to Europe and Asia.

Margaret was given enough time to shed a few grateful tears before Nicole handed her a hastily-packed bag moments before a driver arrived to take them to the airport for a flight to Southampton, England to meet their ship. Margaret lamented that she didn't have enough clothes, but Jonathan promised her that they would shop in Paris and Rome. Margaret quickly regained her composure and kissed her children, not once mentioning grandchildren.

A soft breeze rustled leaves and whispered over Nicole's upturned face. The cloying fragrance of rich earth lingered in the air, reminding her that Virginia had a scent all its own. She loved New York City, but Virginia was home.

But it's not home, she thought. No place could be home without Zachary Regan. His presence offered her peace and protection. But most of all, he was love; a love that was soothing and passionate.

Pushing to her feet, Nicole made her way slowly down the porch and around to the back of the large house. Adam had finished redecorating the interiors and now he was concentrating on landscaping the property. Rows and rows of new seedlings dotted an expanse of what was once barren land. The grass under her feet was thick and spongy, a rising mist turning the carpet of green into an endless sea of heather-gray.

An owl hooted softly and other night birds answered in an unorchestrated nocturnal chorus. Nicole walked through the dew-drenched grass for several hundred feet, then turned and retraced her steps. The golden glow from lamps shone like beacons through the many windows of the three-story structure. She had to pack. She was to return to New York early the following morning.

She saw the tall shadowy figure on the porch. She had misjudged Adam. He had gone to drop off papers to a client; and she hadn't heard his return because she had walked too far to hear his car's engine.

"So, you were telling the truth," she said, moving closer to the figure standing in the shadows. "Forgive me for being nosey."

Nicole paused on the lower step. "What do you want me to do, grovel and beg?" she continued in a saucy tone.

"All right, Adam Oliver Moore, I am sorry."

Adam hadn't moved or uttered a sound, incensing Nicole. "No penance!" she snapped.

"I think both of us have suffered enough, Nikki."

Nicole thought she had conjured him up. She was imagining Zachary was standing on the porch-- that he was in Virginia.

Moisture swept over her body and she stumbled up the steps.

"Zachary?" she mumbled through tight lips.

Zachary moved into the stream of light coming from the entry. "Are you still the keeper of my heart, darling?"

Nicole was crushed to his chest, laughing and crying at the same time. She inhaled his familiar scent, felt his heat as her fingers raced over the planes of his face.

"Zachary," she cried over and over, wetting the front of his shirt with her tears.

Zachary felt his own control break when he buried his face in her hair and held her tightly.

His hands made soothing motions on her back. "Nikki, it's all right. I've come back and we'll never be separated again."

Nicole sniffed back tears and smiled up at him. The moisture glittered like the diamonds resting between her small breasts.

"You're okay?"

"I'm more than okay," he confirmed. "I've come to tell the woman I love that I want to be a part of her life."

She felt her breath catch in her chest. "What are you asking, Zachary?"

He cradled her face in his hands and smiled. "I'm asking if you'd be willing to spend the rest of your life with one slightly-used widower with three children and one neurotic dog? I want you to marry me, Nicole."

Looping her arms around his neck, Nicole rose on tiptoe and gave him her answer. Her moist mouth spoke volumes and when they parted Zachary knew the separation had been worth it.

"Yes, Zachary Regan," she mumbled breathlessly against his lips. "Yes, I'll marry you. Yes, I'll be a mother to your children. And yes, I'll always be the keeper of your heart."

Her world stopped spinning and Nicole pulled away from Zachary, looking out into the darkness. "How did you get here?"

Zachary curved an arm around her waist and led her into the house. "I walked."

She stopped and frowned up at him. "Walked from where?"

"Down the road a piece," he replied, staring at the woman who appeared more beautiful than he had ever seen her before. She had cut her hair again. This time tiny curls tumbled over her forehead and feathered along the tops of her ears. The short hairdo permitted her to display her perfect, flattering features to their best advantage.

"Where did you walk from?"

Zachary pulled her to his body, taking her lips in a hungry, possessive kiss. "You talk too much," he breathed into her hot mouth.

Nicole melted, giving into the heat of the moment. She moaned when Zachary's hand found a breast and kneaded the soft mound of flesh until she nearly screamed from the intense ecstasy.

"Zachary!"

"Oh, yes," he mumbled, his mouth replacing his hand.

"Adam!"

Zachary's head came up and he pulled down her loose-fitting top. "Adam won't be back for a while."

Nicole took a step backwards. "You and Adam planned this, didn't you?"

"I had to see you Nicole and when I called your place Friday night and didn't get an answer I called Adam. He told me you were on your way down here for your parents anniversary, so I just followed you. Adam thought that we needed some time together—alone--so he decided to get lost for a couple of hours."

Nicole visually examined the black penetrating eyes behind the lenses, the sexy dimple in a lean cheek and the lush smiling mouth that wrung spasms of passion from her.

Placing both hands over his heart, she dropped her forehead to his shoulder. "Is it over, Zachary? Is it truly behind you?"

Zachary brushed his lips across her forehead. "Yes, darling. The nightmares have vanished. I'm no longer afraid of losing the women I love. First it was my mother, then it was Julie. And somehow I wasn't willing to gamble on losing a third time. That's why I refused to get involved. No involvement, no pain and no loss."

"You could've told me, Zachary. I would've understood."

"I wanted to, Nikki. There were so many times when I'd rehearsed it, that I was certain I could do it. Then when I saw you I was like a tongue-tied child before an anxiety attack."

For a long moment she held him, registering the strong, steady pumping of his heart. His right hand closed over her fingers and it was then that she noticed the ring was missing. He had truly let go of his past.

Zachary urged her forward. "Adam has given us some time together. Let's take advantage of it."

"That sounds as if you're going to take advantage of

your fraternity brother's little sister," she teased.

"How can you fix your mouth to say such a thing?" Zachary replied quietly.

"Easily," Nicole retorted. "Quite easily."

Chapter Twelve

Zachary sipped a glass of champagne, half-listening to his new father-in-law. His gaze was fixed on that of his bride.

Nicole had changed from a twenties-inspired, ivory drop-waist wedding dress of Chantilly lace and silk taffeta with pearl buttons to a white Edwardian riding jacket and slim skirt. Pale stockings and a pair of bone-colored pumps were flattering to her long slender legs.

His gaze traveled slowly upward to her face as she gestured gracefully to Kathy. A shaft of light caught the circle of gold on her left hand, reminding him of its match on his own finger.

Zachary would have married Nicole six months before, but she insisted they wait; wait until his children had fully accepted her, and she could feel comfortable with them. He counted off the months that seemed to drag by, learning something he hadn't known about himself—he possessed an infinite amount of patience.

Nicole glanced up at the clock over the mantle on the fireplace in her parents' living room. It was nearing the time that she and Zachary would leave for their honeymoon.

Reaching up, Nicole unpinned the sapphire and green beryl brooch on her lapel. She smiled at Kathy. The young girl looked very grown-up at thirteen with her hair a mass of thick black curls falling from a pink satin ribbon. The nautical-style pleated Laura Ashley pink linen dress she wore was delicate and appropriate for her father's wedding.

"There's a tradition in my mother's family that the oldest daughter can claim this brooch." She extended her hand with the priceless heirloom. "I'd like you to have it, Katherine."

"But...but I'm not your daughter," Kathy stammered.

Nicole pushed it into her hand. "Oh, but you are, Kathy. Your father and I are married. And that makes all of us one family."

Kathy stared at the brooch. "What if..."

"What if what?" Nicole asked.

Kathy pressed her lips tightly together. "What if you and Daddy have a baby and...and it's a girl?"

Nicole laughed and hugged Kathy. "Don't worry. I'll have something else for her." *Or him,* she added silently.

Kathy saw her father make his way across the room. She gave him a bright smile. "Look what Nicole gave me. She says the oldest daughter in her family gets to keep it."

Zachary caught Nicole's gaze, loving her without words. "I hope you cherish the brooch and Nicole's generosity."

"I will, Daddy."

"It's time to leave," Zachary informed Nicole in a deep, quiet voice.

She nodded, smiling. "Please give me a minute."

Nicole picked up her bridal bouquet from a table and walked over to where Vera stood with Adam. They were so engrossed in each other that they didn't notice her until she cleared her throat loudly.

She handed Vera the bouquet of white roses, tulips, gardenias. "Take care of this for me."

Vera's eyes widened in surprise. "What do you want me to do with it?"

"Think of something," Nicole said with a smile, winking at her brother.

"Nick!" Vera called out to Nicole's back when she turned and walked away.

Zachary slipped a coat over Nicole's shoulders, his hands lingering on her waist.

They kissed friends and relatives who had come to witness their nuptials.

Nicole was certain she glimpsed a tear from Kathy when they turned to leave. It appeared as if her stepdaughter was a romantic.

Davy and Danny stood waiting to throw the rice they had talked about for hours. Zachary shook his sons' hands, then hugged them.

"Bring back a baby brother," Davy shouted.

Everyone gasped, then laughed.

Minutes later, Zachary settled Nicole on the back seat of the limousine that sped them to the airport for their flight to St. Croix.

He held her hand tightly in his, bringing her fingers to his mouth. "At last," he whispered. "I have you all to myself."

She gave him a sidelong glance. "Not yet. We still have several hours before we can truly be alone."

"I can't wait."

Nicole snuggled next to his large, warm body. "We've waited this long, darling. A few more hours will be what we'll need to whet our appetites.''

Lowering his head, Zachary kissed her mouth. "And after I make love to you I'll have the feel of you on my flesh, the smell of you in my nostrils and the taste of you in my mouth.''

Nicole shivered uncontrollably with his erotic promise. Closing her eyes, she leaned against her husband, waiting for the time when he would make his promise real.

The doors to the veranda stood open to the trade winds sweeping gently into the bedroom. Zachary stood motionless, both hands thrust in the large pockets of an emerald-green paisley silk robe. He stared out at the violet, magenta and mauve hues settling over the island.

Perfection. The setting was perfect; his wife was perfect and so was his world. He had worked through his fears and he loved Nicole more because she permitted him the space he needed to overcome them without her intervention. And in doing so, he'd gained additional strength.

He froze. He felt rather than saw Nicole when she stepped behind him. Turning slowly, he stared down at her. Her skin and hair were damp from her shower.

His gaze burned her flesh everywhere. Her gown was a sensual vision of white satin and lace. Zachary felt a heaviness in his groin when he noted the dark circles of her nipples peeking through the lace.

Nicole's lids fluttered demurely, then closed over her brilliant eyes. Her soft breathing caught in her throat when Zachary pulled her against his chest.

Anchoring a finger under her dimpled chin, Zachary tilted her head and lowered his. His kiss was a whisper on her parted lips before his tongue pushed gently to take possession of her mouth.

His own breathing faltered when her fingers went to the belt around his waist. The material parted and her hand moved over his belly and still lower.

Bending slightly, Zachary swept her up in his arms and carried her to the large bed draped with mosquito netting.

Nicole looped her arms around Zachary's neck, pulling his head down when he lowered her to the sheets, his body following. Her tongue traced his mouth, tasting and savoring the essence that was Zachary Regan's.

"Zack, Zack," she gasped over and over. His hand searched under satin and lace, feathering up her inner thigh, as her breath came in hiccuping sobs.

Zachary was aware of all of the changes: her increase in heart rate, her labored breathing and the heat rising from her body.

Gathering fabric, he removed her nightgown. Minutes later, his own robe slid to the floor, merging with the pale satin in a shimmering pool of green and white.

His own heart slammed against his ribs when he stared at the perfection of her small, firm breasts. His thumbs grazed the golden globes, bringing the darker brown nipples to a pebbly hardness.

Lowering his head, Zachary suckled her and her soft moans fired his blood.

Nicole felt the flutters deep in her womb, followed by a rush of dampness between her legs. She was ready for Zachary's possession of her throbbing flesh. She wanted him to stop, while silently wanting him to go on.

Zachary's mouth left her writhing, burning, mindless with ecstasy. He moved from her breasts, to an ear, down her neck to the pulsing hollow of her throat, then back to her pliant mouth.

His kisses rained all over her body and Nicole couldn't

stop a keening cry when she felt the heat of his mouth at the source of her womanhood.

Nicole did not want the liquid fire to stop and her fingers gripped Zachary's head, not permitting him to pull away even if he had wanted to.

Her head rocked back and forth; she closed her eyes. "Love me, darling. Please love me."

And Zachary did. He drank deeply, over and over, from the moist well.

The waves crashing against the beach echoed the waves sweeping and drowning Nicole in the pleasure Zachary wrought.

It began. Crashing, earth-shattering spasms shook her from head to toe. She climaxed once, twice and then again, each one taking her higher and higher until she was faint from her fiery release.

Zachary moved over her limp body, his mouth closing over hers and permitting her to taste herself. She sighed weakly when his hardness filled her wet, pulsing flesh.

He took his time loving her, thrusting with a determined, deliberate rhythm, reviving Nicole. Soon her body moved in concert with his.

Zachary's craving for Nicole knew no bounds. The feel of her heat, moistness and her feminine scent heightened all of his senses, and his own heat threatened to consume them both.

He loved her. And he never got tired of telling her that he loved her. However, the words paled when his taking of her body became a raw act of possession.

He belonged to her; she belonged to him; they belonged to each other.

"I love you," Zachary groaned savagely. "I love..." The rest was lost in the explosions that rained down fiery bursts of passion as his body succumbed to the release and peace that would follow him for a lifetime.

Their bodies cooled, their breathing slowed and Nicole and Zachary drifted off to a private world for lovers only.

They awoke hours later, famished. They feasted again until sated. It was only then that they found what they both sought from the moment they met: to be keepers of love.

The End

Printed in the United States
17354LVS00001B/58